Masks of Scorpio, chronicling the headlong adventures of Dray Prescot on that marvellous world of Kregen four hundred light years from Earth, is, like all the volumes of the saga, arranged to be read as a book in its own right. Dray Prescot is a man above middle height, with brown hair and eyes, brooding and dominating, an enigmatic man with enormously broad shoulders and superbly powerful physique who moves with the deadly grace of a savage hunting cat.

The Star Lords, mortal but superhuman beings, have a grand design for Kregen and employ Prescot and his Khibil comrade Pompino to perform the derring-do sections of the plan. Often at cross-purposes with the Star Lords, Prescot is now whole-heartedly with them in their desire to stamp out the unholy cult of Lem the Silver Leem.

Down in the island of Pandahem, Prescot, using the alias of Jak, has burned a temple or two, has rescued his wayward daughter, the Princess Dayra, Ros the Claw. They have seized the treasure of an army outfitting to invade Vallia.

Always looking forward, Prescot must face this new relationship with Dayra. With the crew and mercenary marines of Pompino's ship *Tuscurs Maiden*, they are sailing into fresh adventures under the streaming mingled radiance of the Suns of Scorpio.

Alan Burt Akers

MASKS of SCORPIO

by Dray Prescot
As told to Alan Burt Akers

DAW BOOKS, INC.

DONALD A. WOLLHEIM, PUBLISHER

1633 Broadway, New York, NY 10019

The Pandahem Cycle
MAZES OF SCORPIO
FIRES OF SCORPIO
TALONS OF SCORPIO
MASKS OF SCORPIO

First Printing, April 1984

1 2 3 4 5 6 7 8 9

DAW TRADEMARK REGISTERED
U.S. PAT. OFF. MARCA
REGISTRADA. HECHO EN U.S.A.

PRINTED IN U.S.A.

TABLE OF CONTENTS

CHAPTER ONE

Gold

How do you get on to civilized speaking terms with a daughter you haven't met until she was a grown woman, a tiger-lady with Whip and Claw who once sought to rip your face off? It's not all that easy. No, by Vox, not at all easy!

We sat together in the mizzen top, looking aft. Far astern two shining triangles showed where the pursuit gained remorselessly upon us in the quartering breeze. Soon they would overtake us and attempt to board and we would fall to handstrokes in the red roaring madness of battle—but far, far more important than that were these first stumbling steps in building a relationship between father and daughter.

My daughter, the Princess Dayra of Vallia, known as Ros the Claw, could not be expected to become suddenly all Sweetness and Light. After all, she'd hated and loathed me all her adult life. To find out that she had been betrayed and deceived, lied to, misled, and that I wasn't quite the rogue she thought—not quite, but nearly, by Krun!—must have hit her with a shock that might topple less resilient minds.

As our ship, the stout bluff-beamed argenter *Tuscurs Maiden,* sailed on across the Sea of Opaz, bursting the water to a dazzlement of foam, she said to me: "What am I going to say to mother? I feel such a—such a—"

"I'm prepared to take most of the blame there is floating around," I told her. "Most, but, by the Black Chunkrah! not all! You've got to face up to it, too. And your mother shares no part of the blame. Frankly, I don't know how she has managed over the seasons, what with me going off and the children turning into a bunch of rapscallions—well, except for Drak—"

7

"Drak!" She laughed, high and perhaps a little too tensely. Her face—that gorgeous passionate face so much like Delia's face darkened by the undercurrents of character she must inherit from me—regarded me in a wild, self-hurting way. "Drak is a sober-sides! He's so high and mighty and filled with his own sense of integrity he'll—he'll. . . ."

"He's a good brother to you, Dayra."

"Perhaps he tried to be. He did try to speak to me a few times. . . . But I was surrounded by brilliant and clever people who told me—"

"Who told you a pack of lies!"

She did not answer but held out her hand for the spyglass.

"They're catching us," she said, the glass centered and swaying with our movement. "But they're slow about it."

With that characteristic half-tilt of the head and a swift squint up she established the positions of the Suns. The great red sun, Zim, and the smaller green sun, Genodras, the twin Suns of Antares shed their streaming mingled radiance upon the face of Kregen and Dayra wrinkled up her nose and said: "I doubt they'll overhaul us before nightfall."

"The Maiden with the Many Smiles is due early," I pointed out. As the largest of Kregen's seven Moons, the Maiden with the Many Smiles would afford light enough for boarding.

"True. But there will be cloud."

"You're sure?"

"No. But it is likely. Zankov was always complaining about the clouds."

I made no reference to Zankov, the chief instigator of my daughter's ills. My comrade, Cap'n Murkizon, in breaking Zankov's back, had not quite killed him. I couldn't honestly say I wished greatly for the rogue's recovery.

As though the thoughts in our heads followed a similar train, Dayra said—and with a tartness that was not all mischievous twinkle: "Suppose I told this bloodthirsty crew you've gathered around you just who you are? If I told them you were the Emperor of Vallia—what d'you think they'd do?"

"That's easy. They wouldn't believe you. I'm just Jak, or Jak the Shot, or Jak the Whatever Has Recently

Happened. They'd laugh in your face. But, still, if you care to, try it. Tell them."

"And your foxy Khibil partner, Pompino?"

"Well, I'll allow he might believe it. He has heard the name of Dray Prescot mentioned before."

She steadied the glass upon the two pursuing ships.

"Oh?"

"The lord of Bormark—whose coast is just visible to the southward—Kov Pando, and his mother, the Kovneva Tilda, knew me when I told them I was called Dray Prescot. They remain firmly convinced that I used the name as an impostor. They believe I am Jak, for they met the real Emperor of Vallia on an unhappy occasion for them. That, they tell me, was not me. So I think Pompino will take the same tack. It is not easy to persuade ordinary folk that emperors and princesses go wandering around among them—as you should know, Ros the Claw."

"You call me Ros Delphor!"

"Agreed. I merely made a point."

Mind you, young Dayra for all her artistry with the Whip and the Claw, the rapier and the dagger, for all her cunning and resourcefulness, was still not yet your fully accomplished spy. She unthinkingly used Vallian expressions. She swore by Vallian gods and spirits. Down here in Pandahem, whose various nations had over the seasons fought many costly campaigns against reivers from Vallia, Vallians were not welcomed with open arms. She'd chosen to adopt the new name of Ros Delphor. Now, I happened to know where Delphor was, although it boasted but one claim to fame, and that within the boundaries of Vallia.

Delphor was a tiny, insignificant, placid village situated in a pleasant and verdant spot in Delia's Imperial province of Delphond. Its one claim to fame was that, some five hundred years or so ago, the puissant and much-respected Sister of the Rose, Vasni Caterion ti Delphor, had been born in a tiny thatch-roofed tumbledown. As I say, this information would mean nothing outside the island empire and, one has to admit, precious little inside, except to those who cared. I just happened to know through the insights vouchsafed me into the Sisters of the Rose and allied sororities by the Everoinye, the Star Lords. The point was, Delphor was a Vallian name. It had the ring of Vallia. Dayra ought to have chosen a name either more neutral or positively Pandahemic in its associations.

So said I, watching those two bloodhounds forereaching on us, and gauging the descent of the Suns, and worrying over Dayra, and, in general, not overmuch enjoying myself.

"You all right up there, Jak?" bellowed up Pompino from the quarterdeck.

I leaned over. His reddish whiskers bristled, his arrogant foxlike face shone ruddily. I bellowed back.

"All all right. They gain on us steadily."

"May the black flux of Armipand suck them down!"

Dayra said to me: "Do I detect a querulous note in our proud Khibil?"

"Oh," I said. "Pompino's top class on land, and in a fight on the sea. But since he bought his fleet of ships he's turned into a worry-guts over them, coddling them like a hen over chicks, always worrying that something will bring disaster—"

"Something usually does!"

Those sort of laws operate on Kregen as on Earth. . . .

Dayra had only recently won free of her evil friends, and we had had little time together in which to pack all the talking necessary. Mingled with the wondering reflections on our previous conduct when we had met were all the painful readjustments we had both to make. There was no sense in trying to rush all this.

Pompino yelled again, and the lookout perched in the crosstrees screeched down the enlightening information that our pursuers gained on us, slowly but relentlessly.

"I'm for a wet," I said.

"I'll race you down." With that Dayra hoicked a long and shapely leg over the side and started down the ratlines, going like a grundal of the rocks. To do what any self-respecting middy would do, and slide down the backstay, would see me on deck well in the lead. I did not. I clambered down after her and we touched the planks at the same time, flushed and with something of that mad helter-skelter enthusiasm that comes of rapid descents. Eiffeltoweritis, you could call it.

"Ha!" Pompino greeted us with a flourish, twirling up his mustache. "You two have something to cheer you up, then."

"Unlike you, Pompino, who has the cares of a fleet of ships on his shoulders."

"Aye! Well may you mock! Every time I put to sea I am beset with pirates, with storms, with everything to upset a fellow!"

"That's the way of it when you're a sailorman."

No one aboard knew that Dayra was my daughter. She was known as Ros Delphor, a good companion, and handy with a rapier. If those two ships tracking us managed to board, Dayra would be in there, hacking and slashing with her Claw and thrusting with her rapier. She was worth two in a fight like that.

That I felt absolute horror at the prospect, that I heartily wished my daughter was not involved, is only half the truth. Certainly I wished that Dayra was not into all this fighting. But, as this was Kregen and she was a princess, a Sister of the Rose, and engaged on hazardous missions, then what must follow would follow and there was precious little I could do about it.

Captain Linson, master of *Tuscurs Maiden*, spoke in his brisk efficient manner. A valuable man, this, one who while seeking his own fortune enhanced the fortunes of the Owner. That Pompino would see this arrangement the other way around was, besides being amusing, a part and parcel of the relationship these two had.

"We're in for a blow," said Linson.

I stopped myself from the instinctive snuff at the air. For what may appear simple reasons I had pretended to have no knowledge of the sea. This was a foible which amused me at the time I'd first begun it; now it dragged a trifle. All the same, I would persevere. . . .

"You think so!" exclaimed Pompino. He bristled. He took it as a personal affront when the gods of the waves heaved in wrath and upset his insides.

"Green Nasplashurl of the Seaweed Mane will ride tonight, I think," went on Linson with dry relish.

Pompino cast a hunted, a furtive look around.

"Is there no cove where we may shelter, captain?"

"With those two beauties on our tail, horter?"

"Oh, we'll blatter them, good and proper, when the time comes. I'm thinking of my supper."

"You mean, dear Pompino," said Dayra, "that it is likely not to remain your property for long?"

A booming laugh brought Cap'n Murkizon, barrel-bodied, startlingly red of face, fiery-eyed, alongside. "I'll warrant you'll keep your supper down, horter Pompino, if we get to handstrokes with those fellows! By the decaying gums and putrescent eyeballs of the Divine Lady of Belschutz! There's nothing like a little blattering to tighten up a fellow's insides!"

I felt for my comrade. He and I both worked for the Star Lords and carried out perilous missions for them. We'd come to this strange, unspoken, understanding that each was responsible for the other in the eyes of the Everoinye. They might not see it that way, for they were superhuman, mysterious powers who spoke to us through the agency of a giant scarlet and golden bird. But we felt it. For sure.

"The pity of it," I said, "is that this ship is from South Pandahem. Up here in the north—well, what do you know of the shoals, the navigation points, the hazards? Cap'n Murkizon? Captain Linson?"

Both shook their heads.

"We sail without charts here—and that is a fool's pastime." Linson had not suffered to let his view on this folly be known.

"Unless we take charts from some wight or other . . ." Cap'n Murkizon let his words trail off, uncharacteristically.

"From them?" I said, and jerked my thumb sternwards.

The rascally leanings of these rapscallions were proving a joy to me, used as they were in the service of the Star Lords and Vallia. In the fertile loam of their scheming brains the idea rooted itself instantaneously, grew, flowered, and their reactions exploded in a thunderous chorus of: "Aye!"

I was, as the saying goes, showered in petals.

Since the time when he'd counseled us to refrain from fighting the hideous Shanks and then we went ahead to fight them, Cap'n Murkizon fancied his honor impugned and considered he continued on in life with a slur attached to his name. This was not so. What it did mean was that, the Cap'n Murkizon with us at the moment would not, most certainly would not, be the one to mention the odds. He would not point out that we would have to fight two ships. A few moments ago all we had been thinking of was running away from them and taking the treasure we had—liberated was the right word here, by

Krun!—to where we could share out the spoils; now we turned our scheming minds to the question of how best to ensure the destruction of our pursuers.

Well, that is not only the way of Earth as of Kregen, it is a way to gain your ends, or gain your end.

Wilma the Shot stepped forward. She and her sister, Alwim the Eye, had proved themselves fine varterists, who could shoot their ballistae with great accuracy. Also they had fought with us with cold steel, and we valued them with their free ways and their ready comradeship in hard times as well as good.

"We cripple one of them," said Wilma, with firm confidence in her and her sister's expertise in loosing the rock or the dart from their ballistae. "Then we draw off and—"

"Take the other like a plucked fruit," finished Alwim the Eye.

"Sound," said Pompino. "Very sound. Your thoughts, Captain Linson?"

"I sail the ship, horter. I can handle her to run rings around those two." He pointed a casual hand aft. The glint of sail was visible from the quarterdeck now.

No one was fool enough to comment that these two had the heels of *Tuscurs Maiden*. Argenters are built for carrying capacity and for comfort, not for speed.

The two varterist sisters, well-pleased, went off to check their weapons which needed no checking. Between them they could knock over just about anything those two sea wolves on our tail might put up against them.

The rest of our company would be as ready to fight as they ever were. An interesting little problem cropped up as clouds began to build and some of the refulgent glory of the twin suns dimmed. Our two pursuers would surely catch us before nightfall; if the brewing gale broomed in with any power before that the whole picture would change. If the storm held all night as it might well do, we might never see these two sea wolves again. And that, it was very clear, would suit us admirably. With the treasure we had won aboard and crying out to be divided up according to the customs, a fight would at best be merely a distraction from the important work, and at worst might mean we could lose the gold.

"Pantor Shorthush of the Waves holds a personal grudge against me. I am sure of it," said Pompino. He spoke fretfully. Up here in Pandahem they called Shorthush of the Waves Pantor, instead of Notor, his lordly title down in Havilfar. He was one of the armada of Kregen lords who out of spite or mere idleness, mere mischief, send the gales to sink honest men's ships.

"I think Pantor Shorthush may be smiling, if wickedly, upon us, Pompino, for if the outskirts of the gale strike us early we can use them to escape those two fellows back there."

"Escape? I thought we were going to blatter them for charts—?"

"Oh, we will if we have to. But we have more important ends than that." I stared up at the massing banks of cloud. "Anyway," I added with deliberate carelessness, "we can always buy, beg or steal charts at a more convenient time."

"I suppose that is sooth. . . ."

I wasn't about to tell my comrade that I wished devoutly to avoid a fight because Dayra was aboard.

And that reason, of course, was highly ludicrous. Ros the Claw was a formidable fighting phenomenon, well able to take care of herself. All the same, in the brutal slog of a boarding action even the finest swordsman of any number of worlds—and I am not that one—can get a knock on the head and drop into the sea with a splash that ends all. . . .

And, I admit to a fascination in finding out just how good Dayra was. That she was very good indeed was obvious from her training with the Sisters of the Rose, from her exploits, and from the simple fact that she was still alive.

Tuscurs Maiden ran on in her lumpy wallowing fashion and Captain Linson kept casting black looks aloft to match the gathering sky. He was reluctant to take in any canvas. If he did so the pursuers would race up to us; if he did not and the breeze increased with sudden ferocity he could lose a sail or two, perhaps a spar. The situation was tricky.

Down in the Shrouded Sea in the great continent of Havilfar, south of the equator, sailors have to deal with volcanic disturbances almost as often as gales. Down there they call on Father Shoshash the Stormbrow, imploring him through Mother Shoshash of the Seaweed Hair not to destroy them. Up in Vallia the seamen of the superb Vallian galleons call less on the gods and spirits

of the sea in terms of supplication, demanding a live and
let live policy. Vallian sailors trust to their ships and
their nautical skills. They apostrophize Corg from time
to time; but he and they rub along.

Had we been in a galleon of Vallia now, I would not
have been so concerned. As it was, I owned to a lively
feeling of imminent disaster. And this, as you will
perceive, was because I sailed with my daughter as
shipmate.

So it was that when the blue-glimmering apparition
appeared on the forecastle of the ship I was among the
first to leap eagerly for the help promised.

"Mindi the Mad!" yelled those who knew her. She had
helped us before and now she was going to help us
again. . . .

We crowded up. She stood on the castle which, in an
argenter was a real castle-like construction containing
varters and not the low lean fo'c'sl of a galleon.

"Mindi! Mindi the Mad!"

She stood there in her usual pose, head downbent and
her auburn hair shining from a light that never came
from the suns above us. Her pale blue gown reached in
its straight folds to a circle about her feet. Her arms
were folded in the gown.

Yet her figure wavered. She shimmered. We all knew
the witch was not really standing on our forecastle; but
her apparition presented far less of the solid reality it
had shown before. A dark blur of the bowsprit showed
through her, until her blueness coalesced and she was
fully fleshed before us; then the image flickered and
wavered erratically.

Naghan the Pellendur who ran our guards with admirable correctness in the absence of the cadade, said: "She
is having great difficulty. And there is no wonder at
that!" He spoke with a crisp disdain which embraced the
sea and all things to do with the ocean.

The blue-gowned apparition lifted an arm. A pale hand
pointed landward.

We all craned over the bulwarks to look.

A shadow raced across the sea. Clouds massed above
and the radiance of jade and crimson lay low across the
water beyond the shadow. Rimming the horizon the coast
of Bormark lifted jagged peaks.

Captain Linson said: "If we sail inshore I will not answer for the shoals—"

"Yet she clearly intends us to do just that." Pompino tugged at his whiskers.

"She must know a way of safety." Naghan the Pellendur looked decidedly unhappy. He was a Fristle, and it is notorious that that race of catlike diffs are not enamored of the sea. They make atrocious sailors, and are generally not employed aboard ship. Naghan, for one, would dearly love to set foot safely on dry land once more.

Cap'n Murkizon let rip a bellow.

"Put good men in the chains, Captain Linson! Go craftily. If this witch leads us, we can find a safe passage. By the unwholesome armpit of the Divine Lady of Belschutz! For an expert captain such as yourself the risk is not so great!"

The mockery with which Linson habitually treated Murkizon was now being turned back on his own head. It was amusing. The situation itself, also, held amusing overtones. I simply stood back and didn't even bother to take a mental wager on the outcome.

An abrupt blast of wind that stretched our canvas and heeled *Tuscurs Maiden* settled the issue.

We were convinced that Mindi the Mad knew the coast and that she would not send us hurtling down onto rocks driven helplessly by the wind. There was a secure cove there sheltered from the gale. That had to be so. . . .

In the refreshing way of your rapscallion Kregan they would have fallen into a sprightly argument, well-spattered with flowery oaths, before deciding to do what was obvious.

For some unfathomable reason—no doubt connected with my thoughts of Dayra—I was jolted into a memory of the time I'd spent as a kaidur in the jikhorkdun of Huringa in Hyrklana. The arena's silver sands had wallowed in spilled blood and I'd fought as a sworder against horrific beasts and wilder men. In those days I'd dreamed of my baby twins, Drak and Lela, for the rest of the children had not yet visited Kregen. I'd thought, even then, that babies grow up and face their own problems. Well, by Zair! My children had grown up and they did, indeed, face their own horrific problems. The amusing kicker here was that Dayra's twin brother, Jaidur, had grown up to become the king of Hyrklana. I could never have expected that when I'd fought in the arena in Huringa's jikhorkdun!

So, impelled by these old thoughts, and perhaps with more of that old, lowering, black, devil's mask that was the real Dray Prescot, I stepped forward.

"Let us follow Mindi's direction and seek a safe cove and to Sicce's Gates with these rasts who follow us! Then we can divide up the treasure and see each one of us obtains his just share and reward."

Pompino glanced at me with a perplexed look. Then, at once, he shouted: "Captain Linson! Kindly steer the ship where the witch directs. As soon as we find a safe anchorage we can—" here he brushed up his whiskers in a way which said that, by Horato the Potent, he might not know much about ships; but he was the Owner, and he knew a bit of sea-going jargon or two—"where we can drop the hook."

Some of the old sea salts down in the waist laughed at this; but the situation eased dramatically.

As for me—I felt the relief that Dayra was going to be kept out of another fight. She was a trained fighting girl, a mistress of the Whip and Claw. She had sheathed her Talons for a space. Those wicked razor-sharp talons affixed to her Claw that could rip a fellow's face off as soon as look at him, they would remain sheathed if I had my way.

And that, as any onker could tell you, was as unlikely a happenstance on Kregen as anything else. The future would not hold that Sweetness and Light I craved, and yet the darkness would be illuminated by flashes of that lightning that comes only from good companionship and stout hearts and a brave striding on against fortune.

Running before the wind we sped rapidly toward the coastline. Any skipper in his right mind would have nothing whatsoever to do with this madness—running freely down onto a lee shore! Insanity! But we trusted the pale-blue glimmering apparition of the witch-woman, Mindi the Mad.

The moment an upflung headland of gaunt striated rock passed away to starboard the wind moderated spectacularly. Our canvas flapped. We moved on sluggishly in the wayward eddying currents of air spilling over into this wide expanse of sheltered water.

We had way enough to continue and to enter the mouth

of a funnel-shaped bay. The land swept away and upward into mountain crests, and all clothed with strongly green vegetation. A river no doubt spilled down between those hills. The thought occurred to me, idly, that in all probability the water we now sailed was perfectly drinkable.

Islands scattered reflections of themselves, many islands, and flocks of birds, driven to seek shelter by the oncoming gale, wheeled and squawked in the preliminaries of settling down. The shafting light of the Suns lay low and bewilderingly, glittering up refulgently from the water.

Selecting one of the islands we rounded to in a good depth of water off a yellow beach. Here we did as Pompino in his newly won nautical expertise had prescribed and dropped the hook.

"A goodly shelter, this, far from prying eyes," said Captain Linson. He was well pleased. He, it was clear, saw no sense in risking his ship in a combat against twice his number. And also, he like us could foresee the time when we'd come by charts of these waters, honestly or otherwise.

When a ruffianly crew of us went ashore for fresh water and firewood, Pompino roundly declared that, by Horato the Potent, he would spend the night on honest solid ground. A tentlike shelter was rigged, the fires were started, and the ship's cook, the superb culinary artist Limki the Lame, with his assistants, prepared our evening meal. An anchor watch was left aboard *Tuscurs Maiden*, and we had to promise them their partners would oversee their share in the gold.

Sharing out the treasure!

Ah! That was now the single most important fact in all the universe to this bunch of rapscallions.

The apparition of Mindi the Mad vanished to our shouted remberees. We could not hear her speak when she was in this trance state that allowed her spirit to visit us, and we doubted if she could hear us, but being good Kregans we shouted the remberees in good heart. The two pursuing ships might snuffle about these scattered islands all night; we had no doubt that they'd never spot our fires, and if their captains had any sense they, too, would anchor up for the rise of the Suns.

The general opinion, heartily shared by Pompino and the Fristles, was that we ought to make camp here and spend some time reorganizing ourselves. Fresh water tinkled in the brook, game abounded, we were well-provisioned. This little paradise would mightily suit us for a spell.

The chests were dragged across the sand and ranged in neat rows. The men clustered in the firelight. Their faces—well on the faces of the apims, members of Homo sapiens like me, the avaricious gloating could be plainly read. On the faces of those folk who were diffs, races of those splendid people of Kregen who are not fashioned like people of Earth, the expressions might differ. There was no doubt that everyone here looked forward with the keenest anticipation to dipping their hands into the gold and silver. . . .

Treasure!

Well, I in my dour sour cynical old way anticipated trouble. I was right; but not as I'd anticipated. . . .

"We will do this thing according to immemorial custom."

"Aye!"

The proportions to be taken by each and every person were regulated by rank, position and prowess. We had upward of two hundred thousand gold deldys to distribute, made up of various gold and silver coins. There was no rush. This could take all night and still the rascals would be on their feet with a flagon in their fists, gloating. Pompino stood on a chest with the list prepared by Rasnoli, his gentle Relt stylor, and read out the distributions.

Each name was met with a cheer or a groan, a chorus of good-natured banter. The firelight glistened on flushed faces and whiskered cheeks, glittered in eyesockets, caught the rows of jagged teeth. Dayra and I stood together, a little in the background. She had brought the treasure to us, taken from the enemy led by Zankov; she would come into a handsome share.

"Gold," she said. "Ha—the Little Sisters should be pleased."

I did not inquire which particular set of Little Sisters she referred to.

I did say: "In your own time, Dayra, you would do well to return to the Sisters of the Rose. They would welcome you—"

"What do you know of them! You cannot tell me that!"

"I do not seek to uncover the sorority's secrets, my girl. But you could do worse than seek their blessing once more."

"I will think on it."

Now the treasure was being divided. It had all been counted, every last silver piece. The men formed up, and the women took their places. Each one held out a sack, or a cap, a stout wooden box, and the coins were counted out by Rasnoli as Pompino, Captain Linson, Cap'n Murkizon and other of the more trustworthy members of the crew stood by. The process took time. No one minded that.

Gambling began at once, of course.

The slaves we had freed and who had fought with us were entitled to their share. Also we had agreed that the multitude of girl sacrifices we had rescued should also receive each one her share. There was a certain amount of self-serving in this, for as soon as we reached civilization we could unload the girls with a small fortune each. That was the general concensus of opinion. Dayra, I had told and she had agreed, that I wanted to look out for these waifs more particularly. If they were simply cast adrift with a pocketful of gold they'd be dead or slave again in a twinkling.

The share-out went on. The principals, in which number Dayra and I were included, would receive their portions later. The amounts were known. This was not a scheme to defraud our shipmates, merely an example of the protocol in which Kregen abounds.

This amused me. Limki the Lame stomped past, his nose in a flour bag. The bag bulged with the shape of coins.

"By Llunyush the Juice!" he said, coming up for air, his face whitened in splotches. "As fine a sight as any honest man can hope to see!" We agreed. Cooks are important folk.

A vast amount of jollity broke out around the campfires. Wine passed freely. Every man felt himself a king and every woman a queen. There were quarrels. Inevitably so. One or two knives flashed; but it was noticeable that these were mainly gripped in the fists of the newcomers to our band, and the old stagers moved in swiftly to break up the disturbances.

Pockets bulging with gold coins, men and women strutted from the pay-out table to join in the celebrations. If trouble was to come, I was thinking, a few of us retained

clear heads—I was thinking that when the lambent blue
glow spread across the level sands by the water's edge.

For two heartbeats, and two heartbeats only, I thought
the Star Lords were sending their enormous blue Scorpion to snatch me away from this island beach and hurl
me down all naked and defenseless on some other part of
Kregen where I would sort out a problem for them. For
two heartbeats only. . . .

Other folk yelled. Some screamed. A panic movement
away from the beach began and Rondas the Bold fell all
sprawling on those yellow sands that were stained with
the indigo fires spurting from the apparition.

This was not Mindi the Mad.

A face stared out at us from the center of the deep blue
fire. A walnut-crevassed face surrounded by whiteness, a
face sharp and piercing, a face of illuminated sorcery.
Dayra took my arm. We stood, scarcely breathing,
watching. And the hooded eyes in that grotesquerie of a
face looked out in a gleam like summer lightning. Those
eyes saw the beach and the campfires, the carousing
people, the heaps of gold and silver, the broken open
chests.

"D'you recognize her?"

"No," Dayra answered, on a breath.

The spectral image of the witch remained hard and
fiery edged, studying us. The outline of blue flames
expanded. The woman's body rose into view. She wore a
white form-fitting gown after the fashion of the Ancient
Egyptian women of our Earth, banded under her breasts,
which were small and hard and conelike. The gown emphasized the shape of her figure, the swell of her hips,
the slight protuberance of her stomach. Around her neck
a massive circlet of interlocked gold lozenges, studded
with gems, stood out vividly against the mahogany-colored
skin. Her hair was remarkable. Frizzed and fluffed in the
Afro fashion, it surrounded her head in a sheen of chalk-
whiteness—startling and yet in no way incongruous. A
tiara of blinding light crowned her forehead against that
chalk-white mass of hair. The sound of a multitude of
tiny tinkling bells shivered in the night air.

In the fashion of many ladies of Kregen she wore a
glittery linked chain from a bracelet on her left wrist.
But the other end of the chain did not attach to a necklet
on some friendly furry little creature, a doted-on pet, a

warm cuddly bundle—oh, no. That necklet fastened up a
winged, fanged, scaled reptile of hideous appearance, who
yawned widely, revealing a scarlet mouth and serrated
teeth and a forked tongue that licked wickedly this way
and that.

The witch gazed upon us on the beach and we stood,
petrified after the first frantic moments of panic. Not a
sound disturbed the night except the tinny tintinnabula-
tions of the silver bells.

As though an artist wiped a chalk mark clean with a
single swipe of a wet cloth—the sorceress vanished.

No one had the strength to speak.

We trembled in the night air as the sounds of the
crackling fires, night insects, the gentle susurration of
the sea, returned to the normal world. An after-scent of
musk hung in the air. I felt Dayra's fingers gripping my
arm.

I'd made no move to put my hand on hers, to give her
that physical comfort, for I felt sure she would not welcome that, regarding it rather as a patronizing gesture.
But I did look at her, and as I turned my head a man
yelled down by the beach, and then another shrieked in
agony, and a chorus of agonised howls burst out.

Dayra jumped.

"The devil! Vomer the Vile take it!"

She clawed frantically at her tunic, tearing at her
pocket. I smelled burning. She had to rip the tunic off
and hurl it down and jump on it to extinguish the blaze.

All over the beach men and women were leaping about,
yelling blue bloody murder, ripping off burning clothes. I
saw Limki the Lame's flour bag burst into flames and a
lava stream of blazing gold run swiftly across the sand,
molten, to hiss in eruptions of steam into the sea.

So, of course, we understood what had happened.

All the treasure had turned molten.

Gold and silver alike, it melted into puddles and then
wisped and shrank and vanished. We were left, dazed,
smelling the stinks of scorched flesh and burned clothing,
left with not a single coin of all that marvelous treasure.

Dayra said it.

"By Chusto!" she said, her eyes bright. "That gold soon
burnt a hole in our pockets!"

CHAPTER TWO

Pompino simplifies the future

"She may have been a Gonell, for they have white hair they do not cut off."

"She suffered from chivrel—"

"Powdered with flour—"

"The witch! I'd like to powder her with hot coals!"

"With red honey and let the ants—"

Oh, yes, as you can see. The company of *Tuscurs Maiden* was not at all enamored of the witch who had so summarily reduced our worldly wealth, whoever or whatever she might be.

We sat moodily around the decaying fires as the Suns rose. Someone would have to stand guard and the rest would try to sleep. No one felt like doing anything. We were in all truth a most depressed bunch of desperadoes. . . .

"Well," declared Dayra. "I never expected to be rich in this life."

"But that is always an objective, a dream, something one can yearn for," protested Pompino. "Although, mind you, I own my disappointment is in not seeing my dear lady wife's face when I emptied the gold chest before her."

It was in my mind that I ought to do something about the Lady Scaura Pompina, just to give my comrade the sight for which he yearned. But then, being a haughty Khibil, he'd resent at once the implication that he was accepting charity.

That reminded me of something I had to tell Dayra. I drew her a little off and we sat down as Pompino selected off the unfortunates to take the watch.

"Well," she said. "I am disappointed. But, at least, the enemies of Vallia do not have the gold. They cannot pay their soldiers or for their ships to invade us at home."

23

"True. There is something that may make you smile, although I am always heartsick when I recall—"

"What?" She cut into my maundering. I braced up.

"Barty Vessler—"

"Oh. *Him!*"

I felt the rage mounting, and quelled it. Barty Vessler was one of your true koters of Vallia, a gentleman in every sense, filled with notions of honor and duty and with a sense of proportion in everything except risking his own neck. Delia and I had both liked him immensely, for he was upright and honest and if foolhardy of his own person in pursuit of his ideas of honor was always considerate of those with whom he came into contact.

"Barty was a fine—" I began.

"Oh, yes. He told me he loved me and I believed him, I think. But he was so—so—and, anyway, he wouldn't come out with the companions and—"

"Smash up a few taverns? Terrorize a few innkeepers?"

"And so?" she flared. "Life was so *boring!*"

I wasn't going to get into the strict parent bit at this stage. I held on doggedly to what I wanted to say.

"I shall speak of your antics later, my girl. Now I must tell you what Barty has done for you—"

"Done for me? He's dead, isn't he?"

I felt the pang.

"Aye. Barty's dead. When your mother was hung up in chains by that rast Zankov, Barty roared in to the rescue. Kov Colun Mogper of Mursham killed Barty, treacherously stabbed him in the back. It was ..." I held my breath for a moment and Dayra had the sense to say nothing. Then I went on heavily. "Jilian Sweet-tooth has a personal score to settle with Mogper. I believe she has come here to Pandahem—"

"Jilian in Pandahem!"

"We are hardly likely to meet up with her. The island is as large as Vallia."

"I have had words with Jilian. You know her well?"

"We have fought shoulder to shoulder—but she is her own woman and your mother's good friend. Now, Barty said in his Will that you were to have his stromnate of Calimbrev—"

"He did!" She stared at me in genuine surprise. "Barty Vessler left me his stromnate! But—but there must be relations to claim the title and the lands, surely?"

"No."

"But I was not there. You know that tenure must be established. Inheritance has to be fought for."

"I know. I sent good men there to hold Calimbrev for you."

"Oh, yes, I can see that." She tossed her head. "The great high and mighty Emperor of Vallia would send an army to gain land for his family."

"Yes," I said.

She looked away.

"So—you are the Stromni of Calimbrev, Dayra."

"You won't be calling me Stromni here—and do you forget I am Ros Delphor?"

"No—"

"I suppose you are so accustomed to being the emperor now that grandfather is dead. No doubt you are majister this and majister that—it makes one sick—"

This, clearly, was a part of what had gnawed away at Dayra when she was younger. I said: "My friends at the palace usually just call me majis. And there's an interesting development in the services, where they're using jis to address superiors." I couldn't say that this use of jis was similar to our Earthly use of sir in that context. Some time would have to elapse before Dayra learned her father had never been born on Kregen, but on a funny little world four hundred light years off with only one yellow sun and one silver moon and not a diff in sight.

We spoke on for a space and the hurt in Dayra hurt me, also. I hewed to my purpose. Tsleetha-tsleethi, softly-softly, as the saying goes.

Pompino came across looking put out, as he had every right to be.

"This is a fine mess! By Horato the Potent, Jak! I believe the gods have aligned themselves against us."

"Not the gods, Pompino. Just a witch."

"Just a witch!"

"I'd like to know her interest in all this."

"I," said Pompino the Iarvin, "am not often wrong in anything. But I own that when I said this would be simple, I erred."

I didn't laugh; but you had to hand it to my comrade.

"You said, if I recall, that we would recruit a fine gang of rascally fellows, go across and bash Strom Murgon, burn all the temples to Lem the Silver Leem, sort out who married who, and then go home." I counted off the points on my fingers. "We have a few fine fellows; we could do with more. Strom Murgon more bashed us than the contrary. We have burned one temple here, and there are more hungry for the flames. And as for who marries who—"

"Tell me," said Dayra, "about that."

"Oh," said Pompino. "Kov Pando and Strom Murgon both lust after the same girl, the Vadni Dafni Harlstam. Both want her estates. There are the Mytham twins, Poldo who himself yearns for Dafni, and Pynsi who wants Pando to marry her." He gave his whiskers a fierce upward brushing movement. "It is all very simple, as I said."

Dayra put a finger to her lips and regarded Pompino calculatingly. "Simple?"

"Of course."

"And the rest of it. You really do go around burning temples of the Silver Wonder?"

"The quicker they are all burned the sooner the air will smell sweeter."

I made a small sound, a hesitant beginning to an expression of my personal doubts that burning the temples of the evil cult would change the minds of the worshipers.

Pompino glared. "Oh, yes, Jak, I know your views! But if there are no temples—"

"They will build more," said Dayra.

"Then we'll burn them and perhaps deal more harshly with the cramphs who chant the praises of torturing and cutting up small girls into smaller pieces, may Armipand take 'em all into his black jaws!"

As he spoke so my comrade looked at Dayra. His foxy face showed a shrewd scrutiny. No fool, Pompino the Iarvin, as his name testified; I thought he would not penetrate very far into her secrets. He waited a moment, and as neither of us spoke, he nodded. He was about to go on when I interrupted his train of thought.

"We may burn temples as much as we desire. We must win over the credulous fools who believe the nonsense they are told. And that means—"

"That means," said Dayra, interrupting in her turn, "finding who gives the instructions."

By the way she used the word we understood she meant instructions to imply far more than simple orders.

"The priests, the chief priests," said Pompino. "Aye, we'll find them. And I, for one, know what to do with 'em!"

He spotted Captain Linson approaching, and finished: "Well, we'd better see about sailing again. Now we've lost the treasure these sea-leems will be a fine cutthroat crew, I think. Anyone who crosses them will rue the day." He went off to speak with Linson about resuming our interrupted voyage.

Dayra said: "Jak—when mother was chained up, there at the Sakkora Stones. And Barty died—"

"Was treacherously stabbed in the back with a poisoned dagger, girl!"

"So you say—"

"So it was!"

"I had to go off—if you were there—"

"Oh, yes, I was there, with a damned great arrow through my neck. You were concluding the legal wrangle about marrying Zankov—"

"I do not think I ever really wanted that, for all my words at the time. At any rate, I never did."

She looked splendid with her heightened color and the spirit in her; I remembered how she had warned Zankov not to harm Delia. As they say in the Eye of the World, only Zair can tell the cleanliness of a human heart. She spoke in a rush, emptying herself of this particular emotion.

"And Barty? I know it sounds stupid, banal; but tell me, for I must know. Did Barty suffer at the end?"

"The poison worked swiftly. He might well have died from the blow alone; he did not suffer, thanks be to Opaz."

She made a sideways, empty gesture. Down by the water's edge they were hauling a boat out, and splashing, and calling to one another. The camp site was being broken up, and we were due for the off again.

"We had to fly from the Sakkora Stones. I found out at once that mother still lived. I did not hear about Barty until much later. I didn't know."

"And you had no feeling for him?"

"Oh, yes, I liked him, as one would a puppy."

As though it had no bearing on what we were saying, I

said: "I was slowly curing him of his ideals of honor. They killed him before I could—" I couldn't go on. I turned away and stomped off and got my shoulder to a boat and so shoved her savagely out into the water.

"Come on, you lubbers!" I roared. "We've lost one treasure! Let us go and find another!"

CHAPTER THREE

A hairy fighting bunch

Precious little chance we had of finding any more treasure for that day; we sailed between the islands, each one floating on its twin reflection, and entered the mouth of the river, and we saw not a living soul, on the sea, on the land or in the air.

We might have only rudimentary charts of the north coast of Pandahem, and nothing at all detailed of the navigational hazards here; but we knew where we were well enough. Quite a number of the folk aboard had knowledge of the kingdom of Tomboram outside as well as inside Pando's kovnate of Bormark.

The gale, moderating overnight, had not disturbed us once we'd passed into the shelter of that massive uplift of rock, the Sentinel of Bormark. The river was known by two names. This was just another example of the infuriating way in which even simple agreements failed to be reached by two folk, both living not only on the same island but in the same kingdom. Pando's Bormark to the west called the river She of the Mellifluous Breath. Apgarl Superno's kovnate of Malpettar to the east called the river He of the Bright Face.

Fishing villages had to be carefully sited because of the infestations of pirates. Here there had—inevitably! —been two, one each side of the river. Both lay in blackened ruins. We sailed past silently, not caring for the ugly memories those heaps of overgrown refuse brought to mind.

A few birds hopped about mournfully. No doubt the woods were still filled with game. No doubt the insects still sang. We sailed past that desolate scene and if only a few of us reflected on the waste of man's intemperateness to man, most of us were affected by the sight.

Captain Linson said to Pompino: "I cannot take you past Pettarsmot, horter." He'd had that information from one of the slaves we'd freed. The town stood at the end of navigation.

"Well," said Pompino with cheeriness that didn't sit ill on him, "by Horato the Potent! We'll march the rest of the way!"

The traitorous thought occurred to me that we'd hired on these mercenaries in Pompino's home port of Tuscursmot. Most of them were from South Pandahem. We'd picked up a few more folk along the way. But everyone served one end only; each and every single one of them. Oh, yes, we burned evil temples and we rallied around the Owner; but—but! The crew had thought the fortune made each one dreamed of. We'd lost the gold, sorcerously melted into slag that burned our pockets and skins. The salve had gone around, believe you me. So, now, why should any of them follow Pompino into the heart of Bormark? Why should they go to Plaxing to find Kov Pando and all the troubles we expected there? For pay—oh, yes, for their silver sinver a day. But when all is said and done, money has its limitations.

I said to Dayra, whom I carefully addressed as Ros: "Care to take a wager on those who will go and those who will stay?"

She sniffed.

"Typical! You know them far better than do I—"

"Ah, yes, but you have the eye to search out their hearts."

"I'll tell you one thing. That barrel of a fellow, Cap'n Murkizon, will go. And if he goes Larghos the Flatch will go. You won't keep Quendur the Ripper away, and that means Lisa the Empoin will go. Nath Kemchug, Pompino's Chulik, will go, and so will Rondas the Bold."

"You pick a hairy fighting bunch, Ros."

"The two girls, the varterists, they have not yet accepted me. That is understandable. But they'll go and, I think it worthwhile to try to gain their confidence."

I refused to be surprised at her words.

"The ship's company will be split, then. For the crew will mostly stay, I think. Linson will insist, and rightly so."

"I've noticed you do not have many Hobolings—"

"Oh, Hobolings are extremely fine topmen; but *Tuscurs Maiden* is from South Pandahem—"

"True. But Hobolings travel the world like anybody else."

"So that leaves Naghan the Pellendur and his guards."

"They're paid by this Pando fellow, aren't they? Surely they'll earn their hire?"

"Some, I fancy, will not."

"You make me wonder if I should bother to accompany you—"

"I noticed you did not include the lady Nalfi when you mentioned Larghos the Flatch among those who would go. Why was that?"

Dayra put a hand to her hair—that hair so like Delia's, brown and free and gorgeous—and said airily: "Oh, she has no affection for Larghos the Flatch!"

I was startled.

"But they are inseparable! Larghos dotes on her!"

"A man may dote on a woman; that does not mean she is duty bound to have anything to do with him—"

And then, as our thoughts flew to Barty Vessler, Dayra stopped herself. We stood for a while looking over the bulwark as the green banks drifted past.

You had to admit that a girl as sharp as Dayra would spot anything amiss in that sort of relationship. Zair knows, it made me wonder. The lady Nalfi was now a part of our band, generally respected. She kept herself aloof, true; but that was perfectly natural on two counts— one, for the love we supposed she bore Larghos, and, two, for the rascally band we were.

The breeze turned flukey and the river's confined waters meant we had to turn out and put our backs into it. The longboat lowered, and lusty fellows settled at the oars to pull. For a relatively clumsy sailing vessel like an argenter the river, wide though it was, represented confined waters. The flukey winds ruffled the surface and rippled the tops of the trees. Higher up low-flung clouds went racing past, driven by a breeze that scourged inland.

The small cock boat had just brought me back to the argenter from a stint at the oars, hauling upriver, when Pompino let out a yelp. Other people, all staring up with astonished expressions, joined in the exclamations of wonder.

I looked up.

Among the driving masses of cloud a sailing ship of the sky plunged on, driven helplessly. She had once possessed three masts; their wreckage dangled overside in a tangled confusion that merely assisted the wind to propel her onward. She was considerably larger than our vessel *Tuscurs Maiden*, with four decks and high-lifting fore and after castles, with fighting towers above and fighting galleries below. The snouts of varters showed in serried ranks. A single flagstaff reared at her stern, which was squared off and blunt, like the end of a house rather than the stern of a ship. Being of the air she had no need of the robust construction necessary to withstand the shock of the sea.

I recognized her.

She was *Val Defender*, registered in Vondium, the capital of the island empire of Vallia.

On that single flagstaff floated two flags, and each tresh whipped and snapped in the breeze. One was the yellow cross and saltire upon a red field that is the Union flag of Vallia. The other was a solid blue, with a quombora at its center, the flag of Tomboram. The blue flag floated above the red and yellow.

I stood on the quarterdeck and looked up and I held my face in a stasis of emotion, as though sheathed in ice. A Vallian flying sailing ship, captured by the Tomboramin! Dayra started to say something, and I said, harshly: "Can you see anyone up there?"

"There are a few heads peering down," said Pompino. "If they drop firepots on us—"

The breeze blustered the shattered aerial vessel over our heads. Very few of the folk aboard had seen one of these flying sailers before. They were not vollers. Vollers contained power derived from their two silver boxes that could drive them through thin air, up and down, forward and backward, soaring immune to gravity and the bluster of the wind. The flying sailing craft, which we in Vallia called vorlcas, did not possess in their silver boxes all the necessary magical mix of minerals. They could lift up against gravity and by exerting power on what the wise men called the lines off ethereal magnetic force, could tack and make boards against the wind. The vessels of this kind were known as famblehoys in Havilfar.

We in Vallia had made great use of them in our wars
against the Hamalese.

"Bad cess to her," said Naghan the Pellendur. "She is
Vallian and up to no good here."

"Look!" called Quendur the Ripper, pointing. "There is
an airboat!"

Lying alongside *Val Defender* and in her shadow, revealed as the vessels flew past, a voller snugged tightly.
She was not an airboat built in Hamal or in Hyrklana.
From her lines I fancied she'd been built in one of the
countries down in the Dawn Lands; I could not be sure.

Dayra said, "But the Pandaheem do not have vollers!"

I looked at her and spoke up quickly: "Pandrite the
All-Glorious has seen fit to provide us with one at least,
Ros."

She did not put her hand to her mouth or stutter out
some fatuous remark; but she got the message all right.

The sight of solid objects floating in air fascinated
these folk of Pandahem. Hamal and Hyrklana refused to
sell their vollers to Pandahem or to any of the countries
of the continent of Loh. They had sold to us in Vallia, for
we were a thorn in the flesh of Pandahem. Only—in the
old days the vollers we bought from Hamal continually
broke down. That was policy on the part of Hamal, and
one of the contingent reasons for the wars—apart from
the insane ambitions of the Empress Thyllis, who was
now dead and wandering about the Ice Floes of Sicce. No
one would take a wager on how long it would take her to
reach the sunny uplands beyond.

The two vessels, the enormous vorlca and the smaller
voller, blew away before the wind. We watched until
they vanished out of sight among the clouds. Then, as
though a spell had broken, we could return to our normal
tasks.

Yet the aerial vessels remained the subject of talk for
some time. Pandaheem were unused to flying ships. As
to the business that had brought a Vallian here—that
was easy to guess.

One interesting item was that the Pandaheem had
little idea of the difference between a voller and a vorlca.
To them both were simply magical. They were vessels
that flew. I managed to have a quiet word to Dayra—to
her, for she flared up at once.

"I know, I know! But I am learning and soon I'll be as

good a Pandaheem as you! The thing is—she was one of ours and she's been captured! *That's* the important thing!"

"She looked in a sorry mess. That'll be the gale. Jiktar Nath Fremerhavn was in command the last I heard. He's a good sailor. Something else happened, that's certain sure."

"Yes, but what?"

"One thing, Ros. We'll have to act as though we, too, are overjoyed that a Vallian has been captured. We're always in danger. It's no good forgetting—"

"I know."

Her color was up, her head high and her eyes bright. Useless to push anymore, as I well knew. She was my daughter all right, by Vox!

We took turns hauling at the oars, shift by shift, and our vessel slowly forged upriver. The banks proliferated with vegetation of wild and exotic varieties; the birds flocked in prodigious numbers, fish leaped in the water, and the suns shone. Here, between two provinces who were not on friendly terms, the land, quarreled over, went its own way. The king in far off Pomdermam might rule his kingdom; out here what the local lords said went—double. This river, running between the two kovnates, was neglected. Once it was brought under a single control it could bloom and produce amazing riches. Trouble was—who was to rule, Kov Apgarl na Malpettar or Kov Pando na Bormark?

"From what I've seen," said Pompino, giving a twirl to his whiskers, "I wouldn't back either of 'em with a single copper ob. If you want my opinion, the man to put the money on is our villainous Strom Murgon—"

"What!" exclaimed Dayra. "You're backing our enemy?"

She was trying to fit into her new part, then. Until recently Strom Murgon had believed Dayra, with Zankov, to be his staunch allies against everyone including their homeland of Vallia.

"Not with any pleasure, Ros. But I've seen little of this Pando our Jak here knew as a young man. Murgon—well, he'll get more money—"

Dayra, Ros Delphor, half-lifted her hand. Her face looked stricken.

"What is it!"

"Why," said Dayra—"why—the treasure the witch melted, that disappeared—it will—"

Pompino jumped up and down. His whiskers bristled. He looked incensed past all bearing.

"Of course! By Horato the Potent! The devils!"

I must admit that with all the experience we had of sorcery we'd been slow in arriving at the obvious conclusion. That striking white-haired witch in the body-hugging gown, whoever she was, would not just melt down the gold and let it run into the sea, wisp away, vanish. Oh, no. No, she'd collected it up through her thaumaturgical powers. That mass of gold and silver coins once more rested in the coffers of Strom Murgon.

"May the obnoxious and pestiferous odors of the Divine Lady of Belschutz overwhelm them!" roared Cap'n Murkizon. "Then it is all to do again!"

"We will, Cap'n," said Pompino, with a snap. "We will."

"It is not quite the same this time, though," I said.

"True. Maybe I spoke a little too harshly about your friend Pando." Pompino was not going to apologize for a trifling matter like this. "If the chance affords itself of sinking a blade into Murgon, that we'll do right merrily."

Naghan the Pellendur walked up, perhaps a trifle more relieved that the ship sailed quiet waters with green land on either beam. He still tugged at his whiskers with the same nervous violence. "Pettarsmot, horters," he said. "My advice would be that if we sail in we will not be received in any friendly spirit. Quite the contrary."

Pompino said: "My thought, exactly."

"We're from South Pandahem," objected Murkizon. "They won't know we have the welfare of Kov Pando at heart."

His words should not have surprised me. When a fellow signs up to do a job one may sort the leems from the ponshos. Murkizon was a ship captain, temporarily without a command, employed by Pompino. He was not quite the same as any of the other mercenaries. Yet they shared this common feeling. I truly believe that what they had witnessed of Lem the Silver Leem had wrought marvelously upon them. They shared our dedication. Dayra had seen that, too.

"So we land on the Malpettar bank and march in, a normal group of travelers. If we tried to enter the town from the Bormark side we would face more awkward questions."

"That is the best."

So, that is what we agreed. Captain Linson was most heartily pleased and relieved. He would keep most of his crew and they'd return downriver. As to what he did then . . .

Cap'n Murkizon was not prepared to push his opinion after the disastrous—to him—decisions he had made before we fought the Shanks. Anyway, it seemed best to us all to try to handle the forthcoming day or two with cunning and quietness rather than violence. That, we all felt, would come later, and in plenty. Well, as you shall hear, we were right, well and truly right. . . .

Naghan the Pellendur told us that Mindi the Mad, who was with Pando at Plaxing, would probably be able to contact Captain Linson. We breathed easier after that, and many of the fellows were vastly engaged by this use of sorcery on their behalf.

A simple pull on the whipstaff and a hail to the boat's crew were all that was needed to let us glide gently in to the bank. Preparations were rapidly made. We took a great quantity of weaponry, and provisions, and there was a certain amount of scuffling and laughing, for these lads were your real paktuns, dour and doughty fighting men who could let themselves go when the mood was on them. We watched as the sailors who were not going with us pulled *Tuscurs Maiden* out to midstream and then set off hauling downriver.

We shouted the remberees, and watched, and presently were left on the bank, a party of fighting men and women dedicated to two main objectives—if you did not count the paramount objective of staying alive. One was to deal with the vile adherents of Lem the Silver Leem. The other to win a fortune that did not magically disappear before it could be spent.

We marched along the river bank to Pettarsmot, and saw few folk working the fields close to the town. The place was solid enough, with a fortress from which the flags flew.

They left the gate open for us. As we'd trudged along so the folk in the fields had followed on, their day's work done. The evening light lay mellow and rubicund upon the bricks and the masonry. The shadows looked purple under the archway. We walked in, ready to shout the Lahals and to slake our thirsts at the nearest tavern.

A guard consisting of two ranks of spearmen waited, at ease, and their officer sauntered across. He wore metal armor. His sword was scabbarded.

"Llahal!" called Pompino. "We are weary travelers going inland. We do not wish—"

The officer—he was a so-Hikdar—said in a cold voice: "What you want or do not want is not important. Just look up there."

We looked up to the walls. Rows of armored men drew bows, and every arrow head pointed at us.

"Now just throw down your weapons, all quiet and peaceable."

Useless to rage. Some of us no doubt could have escaped; most of us would be shafted. We threw down our weapons.

They marched us off to the lock-up and tumbled us onto foul-smelling straw with water-running stone walls about us. The sound of iron bars clanging shut rattled through the cell and through our stupid skulls, by Krun. We'd been taken up like brainless milbys in a snare. Fine warrior paktuns of Kregen we were!

CHAPTER FOUR

I learn about Ros the Claw

"Well," I said in what I hoped was a reasonable voice, "you can't really blame them. We'll see a local dignitary in the morning and explain. Then we can set off for the interior."

"You're a fambly, Jak!" foamed Pompino. He strode up and down the stone cell and folk drew their legs out of his way. "Onker! We should have come in here with drawn swords!"

"Then," said Dayra in her level voice. "We'd all be dead."

In circumstances like these people display their own peculiar characteristics. Murkizon was all for hitting the first guard over the head and breaking out. They'd taken our weapons away, of course; we were in no doubt that we'd pick them up, or others, in the nearest guardroom.

Rondas the Bold, his vulturine features beaked and grim, seconded Murkizon. Nath Kemchug was perfectly prepared to bash a few skulls to win free.

Surprisingly, Quendur the Ripper and Lisa the Empoin sided with me and counseled caution. They, too, felt that in a civilized country the mistake would soon be cleared up.

"Mistake?" said Larghos the Flatch. He held the lady Nalfi close. "Mistake? The only mistake we made is in not doing as horter Pompino and Cap'n Murkizon suggested."

If we fell to a quarrel among ourselves, well, that would be perfectly natural. It wouldn't help at all.

Dayra had expressed her surprise that the lady Nalfi had elected to accompany us. But, Nalfi had, and here she was, penned up with us between dank stone walls behind iron bars.

The others of our group expressed their opinions. Naghan and his guards were all for a bashing spree. I went across to a far corner where Dayra sat, and plumped down, and decided I wouldn't waste energy arguing over hypothetical actions. Come the morning, and we'd know for sure.

"Then," said Dayra, whom I had to call Ros Delphor, "Then we go out and blatter them." She spoke with feeling. They had taken away the canvas and leather bag in which she carried her Claw. She was clearly concerned over its welfare.

"Aye," I said. "If they will not see reason."

She laughed. There in that fetid den, my daughter Dayra laughed.

"Since when have you ever bothered about seeing reason when you want to do what you want to do?"

"You'd be surprised."

"I doubt it."

We were a little separated from the wrangle, which in the sprightly Kregan way promised to last a long time and be of consuming interest to all involved. A torch cast a spluttery kind of mildewy light upon the scene.

After a time, Dayra said: "You were always gone, so mother said, always off somewhere or other."

"That is true."

She cocked her head and glanced sideways at me.

"I own I was surprised to see you here in Pandahem. Vastly surprised. I thought you in Vallia, seeing about the empire."

"Your brother Drak is doing that."

"So you say. I suppose—" and here she shuffled herself more comfortably against the wall. "I suppose why you were so often away from home was because you were off doing things like we're doing now?"

"Yes."

"I've heard the stories about a devil in a red breechclout leaping about with a great sword—"

"Just stories."

"Folk tend to look over their shoulder when they tell these just stories."

"And," I said. "The breechclout is scarlet."

"Ah!"

We relapsed into silence, each occupied with thoughts the other might, perhaps, only guess at. Water dripped in that noisome place, and little beasties scuttled across the floor. Of food and drink we had none. Our stomachs rumbled and our throats were dry, believe me. But the time passed and we slept fitfully, on and off.

At one point or another, speaking quietly in the glimmer of the dying torch, I said to Dayra: "I well remember when your mother and Lela were off searching for you. You were smashing up taverns, and whatever other deviltries you were up to—I didn't know then, for your mother wouldn't tell me, and I forebore to ask." She turned to face me and the vague light lay orange curves down her cheek. "Wait, Ros—all that's gone now, smoke blown with the wind. When your mother and Lela searched for you—it was during that time we had to combat the Black Feathers of the Great Chyyan—I was frantic with worry. Often and often we've been parted. I don't want those old evil days to return."

She whispered, "I heard about the Black Feathers of the Great Chyyan. A false creed. I do not think it to be much like this Lem religion."

"No."

She settled back. "Now I've tried to find you, I do not wish to be—" She stopped speaking and yawned, and said, "By Chusto, Jak! Try to get some sleep."

In that guttering light I glanced swiftly about the cell. The people were mere misshapen lumps upon the stone. Some snored. I did not think anyone could have overheard us. And, truth to tell—I was beginning to grow tired of this Ros this and Ros that. Well, not so much the Ros, for that is a fine name, as the pretense that Dayra was a mere friend and not a precious daughter. If Pompino knew, he was horter enough to know when to stop his questions.

Then Dayra shifted over again. I could just make out her face in the last of the torch glow.

"The Black Feathers of the Great Chyyan. If we are to enjoy an honest relationship. . . ."

"Yes?"

"Zankov thought he could bargain with Makfaril, the leader. A golden numim hoodwinked him, a lion-man called—"

"Rafik Avandil."

Her eyes opened in a surprise she concealed at once.

"I might have guessed. . . . They ill-treated Zankov and

imprisoned him in a horrible underground temple abandoned for centuries—"

"The ruined temple of Hjemur-Gebir. A monstrous toad-thing of stone, a malignant idol, at the center of the underground—"

"Yes. I imagine afterward many people went to gawp."

"I believe they did." I stared at her, my face in shadow. "And you were there. It was Zankov with a broken arm—"

"How . . . !"

"I saw it. I saw—you!—rescue him. You were there, there, so close, and I wished you well and went on. . . ." I recalled all that old and horrible adventure. "I did not know who you were—except that you were a tiger-girl, powerful and gorgeous, very quick and lethal, and you went away with that rast Zankov. . . ."

"You—saw—all that. . . ."

"Aye." Someone moved restlessly among that heap of sleeping bodies, and I finished quickly: "Sleep now. We can talk over old times tomorrow."

But, before she lay back to sleep, she whispered, "I heard the uproar. I was carrying Zankov along—and we could not find a way out. And then Rafik Avandil was there in his golden armor, raging, cursing, insane with despair and rage, and—"

"It was your mother's dagger. The gems in the form of a rose. . . ."

"Aye. It went through his neck sweetly. . . ."

So I lay back. What one learns about one's children as they grow old enough to confide!*

My penultimate thought as I drifted off to sleep at last was that there would be many more horrific stories to learn of my wayward daughter's headlong career upon Kregen; but I took heart from this, for I felt the trueness of the bridge we were building between us.

My last thought before sleep, as it is every night, was the same; although on this particular night it was of Makfaril's Sacrifice . . .

We were roused out just after dawn by apim guards who kicked us awake. We stumbled into a stone-walled courtyard, blinking in the early light, apple-green and palest rose. We were given no breakfast. We husked

*For Dray Prescot's adventures with the Black Feathers of the Great Chyyan, see *Secret Scorpio,* Dray Prescot No. 15.

about, and tried to spit, and waited while the guards went through their tiresome rigmarole.

The women among us had been offered no indignity, and we were generally agreed that this was a wise action on the part of the jailers of the Pettarsmot prison. We were, for the sake of the Bright Pandrite, in Mappeltar, in Tomboram, a civilized country! When I said to Naghan, speaking in a dry, a very dry voice, that I thought the place was called Malpettar, he managed a hissing sort of laugh.

"Malpettar or Mappeltar, depending on north or south; for us in Bormark they are all tarred with the same brush."

"Well, keep your black-fanged winespout shut about Bormark," rasped Murkizon.

We were herded along to the gateway and here we were joined by another bunch of decrepit-looking folk. They were prodded up from adjoining cells. They had been worse-treated than us, that was clear. Many were wounded and their bandages were all what they had provided themselves. I felt Dayra's hand on my arm; and I did not look at her but fastened my gaze on those poor devils who were whipped and beaten along.

They wore shreds of uniforms. There were apims and diffs, men and women, in that sorry line. Those uniforms wrung a savage gasp from me. Dayra squeezed my arm.

I—I, myself, and Delia, and many another comrade, had helped design those uniforms.

"They're from the vorlca *Val Defender*."

"So I see." I managed to speak the words in the kind of grating hiss a pile of pebbles gives when it slides off a truck, in my old gravel-shifting voice.

She said, breathlessly: "We must—"

"Aye. We must. Now keep quiet and pay them no attention."

As we were prodded along she flung her head up, glaring at me. She spoke softly; but it was a struggle.

"Is that it, then? I see! You will do nothing because no one must know who you are! And there are friends over there—good friends—there's Sosie ti Vendleheim, and—"

"Ros! Shastum! Keep quiet!"

She flinched at my tone, and I blundered on: "If we start anything now we'll all be killed. If we fight now, all our friends will fight—all of them!—and we'll all die!"

"What was that, Jak!" called Pompino, shuffling along. "Something about fighting?"

"When the time comes, Pompino. When the time comes."

"By Horato the Potent! My insides are more hollow than the nine empty bladders of Pantora Hemfi of Promondor! Just let us have a bite to eat and drink before we come to handstrokes."

Murkizon guffawed at that, and a guard hit him with the butt of his spear, and Cap'n Murkizon took the blow and rolled with it—and laughed the louder.

I began to feel sorry for these guards of Pettarsmot.

The two bunches of prisoners trudged side by side only for the time it took to cross the next yard. Here we were shepherded under an archway and so into the building; the last we saw of the aerial sailors of *Val Defender* they were being bludgeoned through the opposite archway.

Dayra would not look at me.

She walked along, her head high, nostrils flaring, her face wild. I managed to crab alongside Lisa the Empoin, for whom I had a high regard.

"Lisa—would you speak to Ros? Tell her how a prisoner and a potential slave behaves. She'll stir up—"

"At once, Jak. You're right. She's acting as though she's a princess!" And Lisa the Empoin wormed her way swiftly to the Princess Dayra's side, and said: "Ros Delphor, listen!"

Quendur the Ripper looked after Lisa. "I think," he said in a matter-of-fact tone of voice, "I really think when I make Lisa a princess, as, of course, I shall one day, she will remember Ros Delphor. If ever a girl should have been born a princess as well as my Lisa, it is Ros."

Do not think I enjoyed suffering under my daughter's haughty contumely. She was in the right, if you took into account only the high jikai kind of headlong glory-hunter who got himself killed half a dozen times. She probably did not fully grasp that the comrades with us now were of Pandahem; they'd fight for themselves, they wouldn't get stuck into a fight with little chance just to rescue some damned rascally Vallians. Ros knew that well enough when she thought about it; at the moment she wasn't thinking but letting all her Prescot and Valhan blood surge passionately into her actions.

The guards bustled us into a chamber where a fellow halted us and formed us into ranks. We stared about owlishly. The walls were draped in deep blue. A railing fenced off a podium whereon stood four chairs, richly decorated. Guards watched us alertly. A woman hurried in from a side door, hitching up her blue robes, climbed onto the podium and sat down in a middle chair. She peered at us with great displeasure.

A small woman, with a smooth yet knowing face, dark hair and eyes, and a mouth that would take off the leg of a granite statue, she used her power without thought.

A flunkey bellowed: "The great and puissant lady Moincy, Under-pallan of Justice, in session." He banged his staff. Murkizon laughed, and Pompino hushed him.

I leaned a little toward my Khibil comrade.

"I trust you have a good, a very good, story ready?"

He swelled. He brushed his whiskers. "Trust me!"

Nobody in this hick town was going to overawe or catch out a foxy fellow like a Khibil, no, by Horato the Potent!

The woman, this lady Moincy, looked down on us.

"You are fortunate that today there are bigger fish to fry. I cannot waste time on you. What have you to say for yourself before you are fined?"

Pompino yelped: "Fined! What are we fined for?"

"You do not have to know why you are fined, only that you are fined. Is that all you have to say? Very well—Each fined two gold Deldys."

Pompino's mouth was opening and closing like—well, like a clever foxy fellow called the Iarvin who had had his breath temporarily snatched from him. Temporarily only, mind . . . !

"They've had a good look at our belongings," pointed out Quendur. "They know how much gold we have—"

"And she's pitched it just right! The slag heap!" said Murkizon, bristling.

Murkizon, unfortunately, was wrong. The lady Moincy had barely started. She wasn't in so much of a hurry as not to be able to spare a few more moments fining us.

Pompino at last got out: "We are honest paktuns seeking employment—"

"Thieving masichieri, more likely!"

"Never! We—"

"Silence." She motioned down and a guard hoicked out our possessions from the chest into which they had been thrown. You may imagine with what hunger we gazed upon our weapons tumbled there. The guard produced a canvas and leather bag. From this he took out and held aloft the shining, ugly, cunning Claw.

"To whom," said the lady Moincy in a voice on a sudden silk soft, "does this belong?"

CHAPTER FIVE

Of fines, songs and fliers

My left arm flew out, as it were on its own, and palm back pressed Dayra away. I held that arm rigid so that she could not step forward, and Murkizon's barrel body concealed my action. I stepped out before my comrades. I looked up.

With my back to them I could put on an imbecilic face, a vacuous grin, a semi-leering simpleton look that I can do so well—as I have all the natural advantages for it, according to my comrades. I stared up happily at the woman and said: "Why, lady, that is mine." Before she could answer I rambled on in a loud bucolic voice: "My comrade, poor Nath the Kaktu, brought it back from some outlandish place, don't ask me where, somewhere beyond the Pillars of Rhine where men have eyes in their stomachs; leastways, that's what poor Nath said, and he won it in a game of Jikalla, he said, although I wonder, for you know how these brave paktuns are, and Nath, he said—"

"Shastum! Silence!"

"Why, yes, lady," I said, and wheezed, and looked up at her grinning like a puppydog.

"And do you know what it is?"

"Why—in course, lady."

I heard the low gasp from Dayra at my back.

"Well, onker? What?"

"Why, it be a back scratcher, o' course, and right handy at bath nights, although it's a mite sharp if you're—"

"You fool!"

"Why, yes my lady."

She glared at me. "You are fined a gold Deldy for being a fool, fool!"

"Why, thank you, lady—"

"And now," she went on, hunching herself up and taking on an altogether different appearance, as though she had sprouted wings, horns and a tail. "And *this!*"

From the chest the guard lifted aloft a glittering star-sparkling silver mask, a snarling mask of a devotee of Lem the Silver Leem.

"Why, my lady," I spoke up before anyone else had a chance to speak. "Poor Nath did say as he valued that there mask above a flagon o' best Jholaix, which as I told him is plain silly for an honest paktun to talk, seeing that it is never and nowise ever was real silver, leastways, that's what poor Nath said, he said, 't'ain't silver, he said—"

"Shastum!"

"Why, yes, my lady."

As I subsided I wondered if I was verily the fool the lady dubbed me, or clever. I had the strongest feeling that the cult of Lem had either bypassed Pettarsmot or not been well-received here. To claim allegiance to Lem, as would have been easy, would not, I judged, have been our best course.

The guard hoisted up the golden zhantil mask worn by the people who slew the worshippers who wore the silver masks. We thought, although we did not know, that Pando had started the idea of having his fighting men wear the golden zhantil mask in opposition to the leem mask. I glared up with my lopsided grin, the simpleton to the life, ready to brazen it out, or to leap—very quickly! —seize a sword and so go red-roaring headlong into action. . . .

"And, fool, this?" The woman's voice purred now just as a big cat purrs—sometimes—before he has your head in his jaws.

"Nath said that was not real gold, lady, and you can see it is not real gold by reason of the bit of brass off behind the left eyehole which I saw at once and told poor Nath and he said, he said—"

She sighed. She looked down.

"Fined three gold Deldys for being a fool of fools."

"Why, thank you, lady."

Somebody at my back was having the devil of a job, spluttering and wheezing and fairly bursting to stop themselves from laughing out loud, long and uproariously.

Grimacing away to the woman on the podium I got a

quick glance back. Trust Pompino! He was in no case to
step forward and take charge of the situation.

But I misjudged my Khibil comrade. He shut his eyes,
squeezed, opened them, took a whooshing breath, and
then stepped out beside me.

"My lady," he roared out, very brisk, very correct, your
upright paktun to the life. "We seek honest employment.
Do you have any openings for guards here in Pettarsmot,
for, my lady, we are all experienced mercenaries, and
take our full pay as prescribed—"

"The land crawls with mercenaries since the wars,
fellow. Go along to that pest-hole in Bormark, Port
Marsilus. They recruit an army there. They will welcome riff-raff like you."

"Thank you, my lady—"

"Fined one gold Deldy—"

"What for?" Pompino was outraged once again.

"Fined two gold Deldys for speaking importunately to
a lady, and two more for speaking improperly. Guards!"

I tensed, but the guards merely ran us out of the
chamber and into a narrow hall where they told us to
wait.

Presently slaves appeared carrying our gear. We checked
it over, grumbling, and found the gold vanished. The lady
Moincy had pitched it exactly—proving Murkizon right,
after all—and there was not a single gold coin left to us.

We belted up our armor and weaponry, and were all of
us in a fine foul mood, I can tell you!

"This place is worse than the Diproo-Blessed Tavern
on pay night," said Pompino. "The quicker we are out of
here the better."

"Absolutely right," I said.

Dayra looked at me, her face rosy with repressed
passion, and then she turned away. Her shoulder lifted
against me.

Surrounded by guards with arrows nocked and ready,
we were escorted to the town gate.

The town of Pettarsmot was just a town. The houses
were neat and tidy, and no doubt the hovels were well
out of the way, the folk were well-dressed and walked
about with a brisk air of business. At the gate the towers
were manned by guards. Flags flew. The Suns shone.
Dust lifted. The hikdar in command waved us through.

"On your way! If you come by here again you will no doubt be more circumspect."

"Oh," said Cap'n Murkizon before anyone could let rip some noise, any noise, to drown him. "We'll be back."

"And what does that mean?"

"Why, horter," I said, pushing forward and grinning that silly sly grin. "We did enjoy your night's lodging—and your supper and breakfast."

His pudgy face blanked with rage, blood rushed under the skin, then Pompino shoved me aside and roared out: "One has to suffer loons these days, hikdar! Never fear. We shall bid you all remberee, and depart!"

Poor Dayra was so wrought up I saw her press her hands together. Her fingers writhed and coiled one within another. I felt for her. But her life was precious, far, far more precious than anything else.

All the same, if these idiots of Pettarsmot thought they had done with me, they were vastly mistaken.

Now it chanced that I'd been wearing a plain blue tunic with short trousers cut to the knee. I strode off along the road, with the irrigation ditch alongside, until we'd passed beyond the first stand of trees where we were out of observation of the guards on the gate towers. Here I halted.

Advancing along the road toward us came the first of the incoming produce from the country, heavy wagons drawn by shaggy old quoffas like perambulating hearth rugs, carts hauled by low-slung mytzers with their multitude of legs. Country folk walked along, children clinging to their mothers' skirts, the men in simple country clothes of smocks and tunics, some with shaggy jerkins, smaller editions of the quoffas they guided.

Pompino at the head of our people passed.

I said: "Do you go on, Pompino. I'll join you later."

"Oh?"

"Aye."

He looked at me. He'd experienced my desires to go off by myself before. He brushed up those reddish whiskers and started to say something, thought better of it, and yelled at the crew: "Step lively, there! We've a ways to travel before we reach breakfast!"

As Naghan the Pellendur reached me I said to him: "Naghan. Would you have one of your lads carry my bundle, please? I'll claim it later, and intact, I trust."

"Of course, horter Jak. But—?"

I was stripping off the blue tunic and cut-off trousers. In their place I wrapped a length of green cloth about myself, unblinking of the color. An old brown blanket went over my shoulder in a roll. I handed Naghan the rapier and main gauche. He took them, mightily puzzled. I handed him the sword, the straight cut and thruster, and he took that, too. Over my right hip was sheathed a sailor knife. That would suffice. Perhaps I'd find a stout stick from a hedge.

The Fristle guard Deldar said: "Hortar Jak. Do you know what you are doing?"

"Yes, Naghan, strange as that may seem. Now go along with your people. I'll catch you in time for dinner."

He shook his catlike head, and tugged his whiskers, but he yelled at his men and off they went along the road.

In the shadow of the stand of trees I watched them, searching for the form of Dayra. I did not see her. I frowned. A quoffa-cart creaked along toward me, loaded with what looked like cabbages. The man leading the animal chewed a straw and wore his hat pulled down. I simply fell in at the tailgate of tbe cart, and Dayra said, "And about time, too!"

I refused to be discomposed.

"Look, Ros, this is no place for you—"

"They're Vallians—and there are others who are friends besides Sosie—"

"Yes, but—"

"It is no use arguing."

So, in a kind of armed truce, we walked back to Pettarsmot where we had been imprisoned, fined—and not fed.

She wore her own blanket in a kind of poncho, and had changed her russet tunic for a blue skirt and bodice. I saw I was going to have trouble with this smart daughter of mine if I wanted to sneak off in the future. . . .

She'd retained her swords, also, under the poncho.

Going along quietly at the tail of the wagon we reentered Pettarsmot. The place looked no different, as indeed, why should it? We went along to the prison block and stopped outside to have a scout around. For all our casual attitude, this was not going to be easy.

"Bash somebody over the head and ask," counseled Dayra.

With a little devil prodding me, I said: "Now if we had a carpet handy. . . ."

She stared at me. "I haven't forgotten!"

"Well, this is how we do it, then."

We found the fellow standing guard at a small side door. As we rounded the corner we both stopped. Dayra gasped.

Out in the center of the parade ground lay the imposing if wrecked shape of a flying sailing ship of the air. *Val Defender*, masts trailing over the side, a raffle of cordage cumbering her decks, squatted like a child's toy trodden underfoot by a careless adult.

I brightened up when I saw her.

"That's more like it!"

"What—?"

"Grab this fellow and let's get inside."

The guard went to sleep standing up and as I eased him to the ground Dayra slid the door open. Light from an open roof spilled down, revealing an empty corridor. We stuffed the guard into a corner, tied and gagged, and padded off looking for trouble. How odd, and yet how exhilarating, to be out adventuring with my daughter Dayra! I thought of the times I'd gone off on adventures like this with Lela, my eldest daughter, known as Jaezila, and I vowed certain vows and if I thought of my daughter, Velia, well, then, I did, and the whole world might stop and still make no difference. . . .

By a side wall in a patio where a well covered by a sharply pitched blue slate roof lorded it we found a flunkey who was only too pleased to put down his water bucket and take us along to where the Vallian prisoners were confined. Usually, when you are on a rescue mission of this nature, it is not as easy as this . . . I watched the fellow in his gray slave breechclout. Dayra paced ahead eagerly.

We heard them before we reached them.

They were singing.

It seems to me entirely unnecessary to say that I'd borrowed the sword from the guard who'd gone to sleep. Now I lifted the weapon, as it were, for all the silliness of it, for all the stupidity of it that it may reveal, I lifted the sword in involuntary salute.

The men and women of Vallia, prisoners, sang.

They were not singing one of the great songs of Vallia, a patriotic paean of glory and valor and nobility. Oh, no. They were not singing one of the rollicking Vallian songs that poke fun at the various enemies Vallia has had to contend with from time to time. Oh, no.

Oh, no. They were singing "The Song of Logan Lop-Ears and His Faithful Calsany." This, in its enumeration of the terrible problems poor Logan Lop-Ears faced taking his father's calsany to market to sell the poor beast, adumbrates stanza by stanza the vicissitudes of folk's lives and mishaps. It provokes, needless to say, considerable mirth.

And the Vallians roared out with gusto, particularly those stanzas that often have their words subtly altered to fit circumstances.

Dayra glanced back at me. Her color was up and her eyes were bright. I nodded. For that moment, I, too, could not speak.

The slave flunkey could. He said: "There will be guards with swords, masters. They will kill you, and me too. Let me go, I beg you—"

"We will not harm you, dom," I said truthfully. "Just bide quietly and see what will be."

There were guards, four of them. They were just about to bang on the door to stop the singing, and then, for the Vallians would not stop for that, more likely than not go busting in to crack a few heads. Dayra leaped. There was a steely, diamond-bright glitter before her. One of the guards fell back, trying to scream through a wrecked face. His companion staggered drunkenly sideways as Dayra's rapier licked back. The other two were barely aware of what was going on until they slumped, and Dayra took one of them, also. . . .

The fattest held the key ring at his belt. Dayra stooped. I stepped back a pace, half-turning, listening.

"Tell them to keep singing, but softer. You go on, Ros. I will see if—yes!"

Around the corner behind us came five more guards, big beefy fellows carrying stuxes as well as swords and spears.

Dayra gave them a single comprehensive glance.

"Come to change the guard. Very well—father!"

She leaped for the door, the key in her fist.

I swung back to face these five who ran on, shouting.

Now if I say I was pleased to see them, you may wonder. I was. The reason, simple enough, was that they carried weapons. My folk of Vallia would need those weapons.

The guards ran up, hurling their javelins. These stuxes flew with varying directions and power, for two of the fellows were apim, one was Brokelsh, one a Rapa and the fifth a bleg. He'd be difficult to knock over. Now it was vitally necessary that I allowed not a single stux to pass me. If one flew over my shoulder it could strike into Dayra's slender back as she bent to the prison lock. So—I caught the first one, deflected the next and the next and the fourth, damnably, nicked me along my left forearm. I used the stux in my fist to swat away the last one—that hurled by the bleg who came from a race of diffs not noted for their hurling ability—some of them—and then I was able to roar on and get to handstrokes.

The tinker-hammer stuff could not be allowed to last. It was all charge, knee-up, dirty stuff, bash and tromple on. And, as I'd guessed, the bleg with his four legs arranged rather like the legs of a chair took the most knocking over. That he was half-dead when at last he slumped had little to do with it.

As he hit the floor a raspy voice at my back said: "Hai, jikai!" and a bulky body crashed past, diving for the fallen weapons. Others of the Vallians crowded up. The singing, which had faltered, now resumed. Dayra joined us. It was all very quick, like gears meshing smoothly. No time for lahals; we had to fight our way out.

There was only one place for us to go, of course.

With Dayra and myself in the lead we raced off. The slave flunkey lay in the angle of the corridor; he was not dead, he had fainted clean away. I commended him to his patron spirit as we dashed past.

Dayra spat out as we ran: "The Pandaheem have been cruel to them! Young Paline Vinfine has been killed. I do not think the crew of *Val Defender* will have much mercy."

"Can they all keep up?"

"Yes. The worst wounded are being carried."

"Good. Is Jiktar Nath Fremerhavn alive and with us?"

We skidded out onto the verge of the parade ground where the forlorn lump of wreckage that was a proud flying ship of Vallia lay abandoned. We stared calculatingly out across the open we must cross to reach our goal.

"Jiktar Fremerhavn was posted into command of *Val Neemusjid*," said a firmly built woman who halted at my side and stared keenly out, not looking at me. "Jiktar Vanli Cwopanifer was posted to command *Val Defender*. He—is not with us."

"Guards," rasped the bulky fellow who'd been the first to scoop a weapon. On the rags of his uniform he wore the rank badges of the Ship-Deldar. "By Vox! I am going to enjoy blattering the rasts!"

"Hold, Edivon! Do not let your rage blind you. We hit them when they reach the shadows."

"Quidang, Hik!" rasped this Deldar Edivon.

So the woman was the Ship-Hikdar, her first lieutenant. I gave her a single searching look. Her face was taut, naturally, hard and lean, with a prominent nose and cheekbones. Her eyes and hair were good Vallian brown. There was about her a calm competence and yet an eager blaze. If I say that one could easily visualize her with a whistle on a cord about her neck, calling: "Now, come along, girls!" I indicate the admirable qualities. If anyone is foolish enough to regard the comparison as in some way derogatory, even sexist, then all I can say is, let 'em rot in their own effluvium.

The guards reached the shadows. The people of Vallia pounced. Then we were up and racing across the open toward their ship.

I felt the fierce leap within me as Dayra was first up and onto the deck.

Magnificent, she looked, wild and free, the silly skirt thing ripped away, her legs long and lithe as she clambered up. The crew followed her and they went raging over the bulwarks and the shattered watch of Pandaheem were overwhelmed. Dayra's Claw slashed and her rapier twinkled, and there were no more enemies holding a ship of Vallia.

Without even thinking about it, the Ship-Hikdar took command. Her orders cracked out. Deldar Edivon attempted to moderate his bellow. Folk dived below to assess damage, and an urchin wearing a rag around her waist came up and slapped up a cracking salute and said: "The silver boxes are unharmed, hikdar."

"Very good, Pansi. Get to your station."

"Quidang!"

That young ragamuffin, that grimy urchin, was probably a high-born-noble lady of Vallia learning her craft as
an aerial sailor. This woman, this Ship-Hikdar, knew
her business. I watched as everything that should be
done was done. Walking slowly across the deck I looked
down on the opposite side. At once I was galvanized into
fresh action.

Down there, snugged in alongside the vorlca, the slender petal-shape of the voller lay quietly waiting for me to
leap down and take her into the air.

"Ros!"

She ran up. "Yes?"

I nodded over the side. Dayra looked.

"Oh, yes!"

The flying sailing ship moved under me. Duty person-
nel were at the levers of the silver boxes, drawing them
closer together so that the power inherent in the minerals in one box and the mysterious substance cayferm in
the other could exert their force and lift all that solid
bulk up into the air as light as thistledown. The raffle of
masts and rigging clattered and groaned as it swung
inward and upward as we rose. That could all be cut
away later.

Without hesitating I jumped onto the bulwark and
took a flying leap out into thin air.

I hit the deck of the voller and staggered and was up,
sword in fist, searching for guards.

Dayra landed beside me, fleet, sure-footed, her Claw a
diamond-glitter.

"No guards."

We were alone on the voller—then half-a-dozen folk
dropped down. A lad looked about wildly. I said to Dayra:
"We'd better—"

She was into the small steering cabin amidships before
I'd framed my thought. The aerial sailors might know
how to fly a sailing ship; they might not know how to
pilot an airboat.

We lifted away as Dayra manipulated the control levers.
Down below on the parade ground soldiers were running
out, many of them. They were foreshortened figures,
glinting with steel and bronze, and they could not touch
us.

A girl wearing a Claw came across to me. She wore

precious little else; but on the scrap of red cloth over one shoulder the embroidered representation of a rose glowed in colored silks.

"I can fly an airboat," she said. There was no blood on the talons of her Claw. "Do you know Ros the Claw?"

When folk ran below to sort out their possessions and to make sure the ship was sound, this girl had seized up her Claw from its hiding place. No doubt she was sorry the fight was over before she could use it.

"Yes. You do?"

She drew herself up.

"I am the lady Royba ti Thamindensax."

"Then Llahal and Lahal, lady. Pray, tell me the name of your Ship-Hikdar and what happened to your Jiktar."

She eyed me. That she felt puzzlement was clear. I did not know her. Of her town, yes, I had heard but never visited. By Vox! An emperor can hardly visit all his towns in one lifetime. We were lifting up now, matching speeds and courses with *Val Defender*. The breeze had veered in the night and we floated along splendidly. Then Dayra popped out of the steering cabin, and through the ports I could see a lad at the controls. I hoped he knew what he was doing! Dayra walked up to us, and she was smiling.

She began unstrapping her Claw. She nodded to the lady Royba's steel bright Talons. "I see you didn't have a drink, Royba."

"That Sosie!" Royba was obviously in a truculent frame of mind. "She beat me to a weapon—but I did kick a damned Pandaheem where he will be sore for a sennight!"

The ships sailed on, suspended between earth and sky.

Royba gave me that puzzled look again. "This great hulk tells me he knows you, Ros. Is that—?"

"Jak? Oh, yes, he knows me—or thinks he does."

I said, "I was inquiring after the name of the Ship-Hikdar, and what happened to the captain—"

"That lady was Vylene Fynarmic of Fallager."

I knew of Fallager, it was a prosperous town up in Turko's kovnate of Falinur.

"As for the captain, Vanli Cwopanifer was—was—" Here Royba glanced around as though seeking the right words. "We were caught in the gale and a spar fell and crushed his head. He was—he was insistent upon maintaining command. Yet it was clear to all of us that he was makib, and this insanity led him into strange actions."

This is, as any first lieutenant, any ship's officer will tell you, a horrible predicament. Cwopanifer had kept up a string of orders, the gale had broomed upon them, the ship had lost her spars and her masts, and then the damned Pandahem voller had leaped on them. It had all been over before most of the crew were aware.

Looking up to the rearing side of the flying sailing ship, I could see the hands already hard at work. They were carefully cutting the tangled lines and hauling spars and yards inboard. If I knew my sailors of Vallia they'd be jury-rigged in no time. I turned to Dayra.

"Ros. Can you take command here? I must go across to have a word with the lady Vylene Fynarmic."

"Of course. And tell Sosie from me she is getting fat." Dayra laughed. "No. Better not. Her Claw is ferocious!"

"This Ship-Hikdar," I began. "Is she—?"

"No." Ros shook her head. "She is a Sister of the Sword."

"And they're a right tearaway bunch!" I said, whereat Dayra looked at me as though demanding to know how I presumed to such knowledge of any secret society of women.

She went into the steering cabin to conn the voller herself as we rose above *Val Defender*'s deck. I slid down a rope and dropped exactly plumb less than three feet from Vylene Fynarmic.

She looked at me calmly.

"I believe we owe our escape to you and to Ros the Claw," she said in that firm hard voice. "You have my thanks, sincerely. Although," she added matter-of-factly, "we were ourselves maturing plans for a break. Those cramphs would not have held us for long."

"That is true, lady—" I was saying.

She interrupted. "I am told you are called Jak. Can you hand, reef and steer? We can use you aboard."

"I am not exactly at liberty at the moment—"

"Nonsense! You're a Vallian. Well, then. That is settled. Report to the Ship-Deldar. He will post you to a watch."

"But—"

"That is enough, Jak! We are an emperor's ship!"

It had to happen, I suppose, sooner or later.

A strapping fellow clad only in a red breechclout was

lustily hauling on a spar as it was angled inboard. The jagged end lashed and he staggered back into me. I caught him and stood him up on his feet. He turned, already shouting his thanks. He was florid, handsome, with bright eyes. He saw me. He knew me. I knew him.

"Majister!" At once, crack, up he went into that rigidity of attention the old hands can always muster.

"Majister! Lahal and Lahal!"

"Lahal, Nath the Cheeks," I said. And then, and I shouldn't have but I couldn't help it, I said: "And now I suppose everyone will know I'm the blasted emperor."

CHAPTER SIX

"The Emperor of Vallia is aboard!"

"The emperor!" The buzz went around faster than the wine cups on pay night. "The emperor—the Emperor of Vallia is aboard!"

You had to give this lady, Vylene Fynarmic, full credit. Oh, she was a splendid person! A Sister of the Sword, first lieutenant of a proud sailing ship of the air out of Vondium. She looked me straight in the eyeball.

She said: "I give you the lahal, majister." Then, still in that same hard voice: "So you are Dray Prescot."

She stood there on her own deck, in command, and I had some inkling of what must be in her mind. She saw Nath the Cheeks standing as stiff as a lance at our side.

"You! Nath the Cheeks! Get the lead out! About your business, you fambly, and no lollygagging!"

He was about to rap out a reply when I said in a carefully neutral tone: "Oh, Nath the Cheeks and I are old campaigners. We were together in *Vela* at the Battle of Jholaix. Nath was a nipper, then."

He bellowed: "Quidang, majister!" and fairly bolted back to putting his weight into shifting the splintered spar . . . Vylene looked after him with a grim set to her jaws.

She turned to me. "You had best come below, majister. They are fixing my cabin last, when we are airworthy once more. But I can find you a stoup."

"When," I said as we descended the companionway, "did you last eat?"

"Just before we were captured."

"Then everyone is starving?"

"When the ship is ready to fly, then we will eat."

I had to agree. But my insides were railing at me like a pack of bloodthirsty werstings.

59

She found a bottle and, at least I could slake my thirst. She wore the rags of her once-proud uniform. The breeches were tattered, and the bodice was ripped. There were bruises on her shoulders. Her rank insignia had been torn off.

"What grade of Hikdar are you, lady?"

"Ley-Hikdar, majister."

She was four rungs up the ladder of promotions within the Hikdar grade; when she reached zan, ten, she might become a Jiktar. Now we had latterly amended the rank required to command the larger ships of the air. Once an ord-Hikdar could command a large flier. This had bothered me, used as I was to the idea of a person commanding a regiment of soldiers being of the same rank as a person who commanded a goodly sized ship. So, now, Jiktars commanded the great sailing fliers of Vallia.

I said: "I cannot promote you immediately to Jiktar, lady, much though I would wish to do so. The Lord Farris has final jurisdiction in the Air Service. But I can and do right gladly promote you to ord-Hikdar. At once."

She took that calmly, with a grave nod of her head. Strong-willed, resolute, she knew what she was about.

"Thank you, majister."

She told me a little more of the terrible time when the late captain had gone insane, and the Pandahem voller had bounced them. Any sailing ship, whether of the sea or the sky, has always to be particularly cautious of a powered vessel. I tried to lighten the tone of these proceedings.

"Well, you can see now that I am unable to sign on with your ship's company. I have things I must do here."

"Of course."

"I would be grateful if you would furnish me with pens and paper. Now I have the opportunity, I will write letters. I would ask you to deliver them for me."

"With pleasure."

So, down I sat at her desk, with pens and much of the superior Kregan paper, and wrote. To whom I wrote and what I wrote will, in general, be obvious. I wrote cautioning Drak that armies were being raised in Pandahem against him in southwest Vallia, which he knew, and went on telling him much of what had occurred, and that he could rejoice that his sister had. . . . At that point I fell to chewing the end of the pen and staring vacantly about the ruined cabin. That Dayra had reformed, seen the error of her ways, rejoined the fold? That was not quite as we saw it.

In the end I wrote that Dayra worked actively for Vallia and that the great rascal Zankov had suffered a broken back, and if he was not dead then the spirits of Hodan-Set had missed their mark. Also, I told Drak that he must summon regiments of our best from Hamal. Down there we had been triumphant; now it was up to the Hamalese to work out their future. I would write, as well; but if Drak was to be Emperor of Vallia—as he was, as he was, the stubborn prideful fellow!—then he had to show Vallia and the world that he was the emperor.

After a dozen or so letters Vylene came in to see how I was getting along. She carried a pewter plate on which reposed four exceedingly hard and gritty biscuits. She put the plate down with a clatter on her desk.

"I decided we should all take a short breather and have something to eat. Some of my girls are faint with hunger."

With perfect composure, I said: "I give you thanks, lady." The way I spoke, the cut of my jib—both gave me intense pleasure. I'd remained calm, cool, perfectly polite. By Djan! That, I tell you, was a great victory!

In one corner of the cabin stood a brightly painted wooden tub with an earthenware inset, filled with good rich earth of Vallia. A pathetic-looking stump stuck up from the middle. She saw my glance.

"Those devil-spawned rasts of Malpettar took all our palines, and cut down my bush."

About to make a reply that, I felt, could not be the right one—for any ship's company sailing without palines to suck and chew on and to find the surcease those remarkable berries can bring is a ship's company in deep trouble, I was saved by Dayra's breathless entry. I stood up.

With all the cracking relish of a ship's captain, Vylene snapped out: "You do not enter here without knocking and waiting, Ros the Claw! Now go—"

"To hell with that! We're all starving—and all we get is this!" She threw a biscuit onto the desk. "Hard tack! Weevilly biscuits and no palines!"

Vylene handled herself well.

"Go away at once, Ros the Claw, and I will forget this

incident. You are subject to naval discipline aboard my ship. If you have come to appeal to the emperor—" Here she half-turned to look at me, and I fancied the gleam of a tinge of uncertainty caught at her.

At once I said: "The lady Vylene commands here, Ros."

"But my guts ache!"

"As do everyone's. We shall be leaving soon. Now—"

Dayra simply turned around and rushed from the cabin.

Not prepared to continue this scene, I sat down again. What Vylene was thinking of my choice of traveling companions made uncomfortable reflections. It was clear that the alias of Ros the Claw well-concealed the identity of the Princess Dayra. As it should do, of course. . . .

Vylene did say, being human: "These Rosy ones, beloved of Dee Sheon. I must crave your forgiveness, majister."

I said, "If I write to the empress, can you make arrangements to deliver the letter into the right hands?" This was an appropriate moment for the subject.

She looked at me, a strong, competent, firm-faced woman in her rags of uniform.

"I am of the Sisters of the Sword. I will call Sosie ti Vendleheim for you."

I nodded and sat down to the sweetest writing task any man may have in two worlds. Sosie came in and stood quietly waiting. She was just such a Sister of the Rose as so many of them were, lithe and limber, flushed with the graciousness of youth and high spirits, wearing her tatters with panache and with the marks of hard toil upon her. When I had finished I turned and said: "Sosie."

"Majister."

"I entrust to you this letter for the Empress Delia. You, I believe, will see it delivered safely."

"As Dee Sheon is my witness."

As she spoke she made that small secret sign. I nodded, satisfied, and handed the sealed packet across.

When she had gone I stood up and stretched and said to Vylene: "I thank you for your courtesy, lady. Now I must be about my business."

"You will take the flier?"

"Aye, Vylene. Aye, I will take the flier. She will be invaluable." Then I outlined some of what was going on across in Port Marsilus, and finished: "So they continue to recruit an army there to invade southwest Vallia."

"We are on patrol against just such a threat."

"Good. But you'll be sailing for Vondium directly."

"Yes. The yards will soon refit us."

I said: "One last boon before I go." I touched the green cloth about my waist. "Have you a length of scarlet cloth in exchange for this?"

Well, that was swiftly provided.

Out on deck I saw Dayra with her head down talking to Sosie ti Vendleheim. My Val! but they looked splendid! As I walked across ready to go overside into the voller Dayra looked up. Sosie moved away, discreetly, stuffing a packet into the remnants of her russet tunic. Dayra smiled at me.

"Well, Jak! And are you ready now?"

"Quite ready. You?"

"Oh, aye," and here she put the little finger of her left hand into her mouth and wriggled the nail around her teeth.

"Didn't your mother ever tell you—?" I began.

"Yes. But you know how roast ponsho gets between the teeth!"

"You little minx!"

She laughed and hoicked a leg up and so slid down into the voller. When folk's insides sound as cavernous as a bat hell then there are tricks aboard a ship to provide the necessaries. . . . I was still sharp set—sharp set! I was starving. But young Dayra had gorged good roast ponsho. . . .

The folk crowded to the bulwarks to look on us as we shot off, waving and calling the remberees. *Val Defender* was already in process of resuming some semblance of a fighting vessel of the air. Her crew were in good heart. I settled back as Dayra at the controls sent the voller slicing through the bright air of Kregen. If a man can ever be content, which by nature he cannot, I suppose that was a moment of minor contentment as Dayra turned and extended a hand.

"Here."

I took the wrapped bundle, a yellow cloth folded over, and unwrapped it, and so looked at a chunk of roast ponsho, a heel of bread and a dip of butter. The ponsho was cold; but it was superb. Eating, I looked at Dayra, and out across the cloud-castled sky, and sighed, and chewed. Life, life. . . . A funny old business, by Zair!

She said with an abruptness that revealed her indecision: "I am glad you wrote to mother—"

"I would not have thought Sosie would tell you that."

"Why not? I sent a letter, also—"

"I see. So Sosie knows—"

"Well, of course! We went through Lancival together."

"Then I am glad you wrote to your mother. She has been through perilous times since I last saw her. The quicker we can settle this affair of Pando's up, and sort out that army in Port Marsilus, and burn a few more temples to Lem the Silver Leem, the quicker we can go home."

She regarded me with an odd expression.

"You are the emperor. What really keeps you here? You could easily fly home directly, now—why not?"

She knew nothing of the Star Lords.

Obscurely, not fully certain, I felt this was not the time to tell her of the Everoinye. That would come. Instead, I said: "It is a matter of plain common sense. If we can prevent the army sailing, or hurt it in some way, we fight for Vallia."

"That is true."

"And this flat slug King Nemo of Tomboram. Now if we can handle him aright he might be more friendly—"

She fired up. "Friendly! I'll tell you what we should do with this flat King Nemo. We should chuck him out and get someone else in—your friend Pando, perhaps?"

"The thought had occurred to me. But—"

"But what?"

"Life is not as easy as the Shadow Plays, or the Farces they knock about in the Souks of Lanterns—"

"I know that!"

Well, she did, she did, as I could testify. . . .

I talked to her for a time as we drove on southward through thin air about the greater problems of Paz, our grouping of islands and continents. She shared the general aversion and horror everyone felt about the Shanks who raided us. We talked companionably, and I felt these recent adventures had helped to bring us at least a little closer together.

Following the road, we passed over forests and open areas and just about the time we calculated, working on the assumption of speed of Pompino's party, we spied them trudging along below. They were all looking up and pointing and already unslinging their weapons. We had taken in the flags of Tomboram, for this was a king's ship, and mightily unusual for Pandahem. We leaned over and waved.

"Hai! Pompino!" I bellowed. "Are your feet sore?"

"Jak! You're the greatest unhanged rascal that ever—"

So, amid the shouts of lahal and the uproar we landed. Soon, with everyone loaded aboard, up we soared, on course for Plaxing, Kov Pando, and what the future might bring of disaster or triumph.

CHAPTER SEVEN

We name *Golden Zhantil*

"Clearly," said Kov Pando, "the airboat will have to be returned to the king. I'm in trouble enough as it is. He was telling me the last time I had civil words with him of how he had negotiated the purchase of an airboat from the Dawn Lands. Mighty proud he is of it. Armipand the Malignant will not spare any horrors for the malefactors who stole it." He glared at me in a most stern fashion.

Pompino burst out most wroth: "But, kov! We cannot send it back! Anyway, we have named the airboat *Pride of Bormark*."

I said, "Anyone who takes the airboat back to King Nemo is likely to be thrown from her deck, very high in the air, or, talking of air, he may find an airgap between head and shoulder blades."

"Too right!"

We sat at Pando's high table in his great hall in his steading of Plaxing. We had eaten until we could burst. The samphron oil lamps gleamed. A party of musicians twiddled their instruments, waiting for the kov to give them leave to begin. Because a Kregan kov is like and yet not quite like an Earthly duke, some of his functions appear odd. As for young Pando himself, well, he worried me. His sharp alert face with the jutting beard, the intelligence in his eyes, as the popular conception goes, the marks of authority about him might have reassured me; but his irritability of manner, the way his left hand kept rubbing over the pommel of his sword, the way his energies appeared almost manically directed, yes, as I say, young Pando worried me.

We had not yet seen his mother, Tilda of the Many Veils, and everyone knew this was because by this time

in the evening she was lushly into her third, or fourth,
bottle and would not be disturbed for an earthquake.

Pando had greeted us kindly. He was a great lord,
even if he was for a moment in disgrace and in what
amounted to hiding. He'd been disgraced before and had
won back into the king's favor. But my comrades were
aware that Pando was a kov, one of the great ones of the
world. Also, we had been very swift to tell him that we
held no allegiance to the Silver Wonder, and were aware
that he had joined the worshipers of Lem only so as to
strike at his cousin, Murgon Marsilus.

As for Plaxing itself, it was a fine estate set in connected clearings in the forests, run by a curmudgeonly
old fellow called Mankar the Horn, an Ift, and although
the place was just a lord's estate, used for hunting as
much as produce, it was unlike the other hunting lodges
and estates I have seen in other parts of Kregen. One
could scarcely expect a hunting lodge in, say the country
inland of Magdag, or an estate in Hamal, to be the same
as a similar place in Pandahem. Yet the similarities
existed as well as the differences.

Pando said, "The airboat will have to go back to the
king, and there's an end to it."

Pompino scrubbed up his whiskers. He had eaten and
drunk well. "The airboat was lost from Malpettar, kov.
No one knows who stole it—"

Almost, I was about to break in with: "Liberated—"

I halted myself. Dayra glanced at me, and smiled, and
I warmed to her. If young Pando got ideas in Dayra's
direction I'd have to think on. Of course, she was a grown
woman and mistress of her own fate, as far as anyone
can be on Kregen. That would be for later.

A lively fellow with clear eyes and curly hair, dressed
carefully and yet with a soberness to the cut of the
clothes, leaned forward. "But, you said there were Vallians
in the town. What happened to them?"

Dayra spoke easily, holding an apple in one hand, the
fruit shining and ripe and ready for the crunch of white
teeth.

"I believe they managed to escape. There was a great
deal of confusion at the time."

"There!" exclaimed this young fellow, who had been
introduced as Poldo Mytham, taking an interest in the

argument. "You see! The loss of the airboat will be blamed on them!"

The buzz of agreement rippled around the high table. They were free and easy among themselves, I'd noticed, except when Pando spoke. Then the strained attentive silence was close to embarrassment.

Poldo seldom took his eyes off the lady Dafni Harlstam, who sat at Pando's right. She talked—well, she talked all the time so that in the end you tended to be able to carry on with other conversations and interests without actually hearing her—and as well as talking she did not look particularly happy. She'd been rescued from the evil clutches of Strom Murgon Marsilus and brought here. Pando was determined to marry her for her estates, Murgon wanted her for the same reason, only poor Poldo wanted her for herself.

Across from him his twin sister, Pynsi, a girl who looked withdrawn, with pale hair banded about her head, seldom took her eyes from Pando, as her brother seldom left off looking at the vadni at Pando's side. It was all a conundrum.

Pando said, "Are you questioning my orders, Poldo?"

"What—? No, no, kov, of course not!"

"Oh, Poldo!" breathed Pynsi.

"I say the airboat goes back to the king. You, Poldo, can take it back."

Pynsi looked stricken.

I pushed my wine cup away across the table. I said: "That will not be necessary. The airboat which once belonged to King Nemo no longer is his. She belongs to me, to Ros Delphor, and to me. To no one else. We say what will happen to her."

"Aye," said Dayra into the shocked hush. "And we're not giving her back to that fat slug Nemo."

Well! I can tell you! A right royal shindig began then.

I had the shrewdest of suspicions that all Pando's people, all his paktuns and Ifts, would not have stood against Pompino's crew had it come down to handstrokes. For, make no mistake, Pompino was using Pando for his own ends just as were the rest of our cutthroat band.

Over the hubbub Pando glared at me. Now, remember, he'd known me when he was a young lad, when Inch and I had taken back his kovnate for him from Murgon's rascally father who had usurped the title. He knew I'd

called myself Dray Prescot, and thought I'd used the
name aping the man who was to become the emperor of
Vallia. He thought I was Jak. But Dray Prescot or Jak,
Pando knew that I'd stand no nonsense from him in
these latter days. I'd told him. Had I been firmer with
him when he was a lad he might not have turned out as
he had, his mother, Tilda the Beautiful, had held my
hand to both their griefs.

So, he spoke up. Instant silence fell.

"Very well, Jak. I agree the airboat is your stolen
property. This means I cannot accept you as a guest. If
you keep the airboat you must leave—or I will arrest you
and send you and that woman in chains to King Nemo."

Cap'n Murkizon said: "I am weary of walking everywhere. I prefer to sail in a ship, even if she flies in the
sky." He did not mention his Divine Lady of Belschutz,
and he made his position perfectly plain. Larghos the
Flatch, instantly, agreed. So did the others.

The green-clad Ift, sitting along from me, who had not
so far taken a great interest in the conversation, by
reason of his continual baiting of a tiny tump serving
girl, leaned forward.

"Better if you left at once, then, Jak," said Twayne
Gullik.

I regarded him. His tall pointed ears stuck up almost
past the crown of his head. His narrow slanted eyes
conveyed that devious look that so marks Ifts, a wayward folk, at home in the forests, clad all in varying
tones and shades of green. This Twayne Gullik was the
castellan of Pando's palace in Port Marsilus. He'd taken
the kovneva Tilda into hiding here, taken her away from
Pompino and the crew of *Tuscurs Maiden*. We fancied he
was a man who backed both ends against the middle and
we trusted him as far as we could throw a dermiflon.

"Far better, Gullik," I said, knowing he did not like
this bald use of his name. "The problem over that easy
course of action is that Kov Pando is in some trouble and
as we are his friends we must rally round."

Some folk took that well, some ill, and Cap'n Murkizon
laughed, and poured more wine.

Pando slouched back in his high chair. The people
around the table rattled and chattered away, and in
all this talk there was precious little of any planning.
And Pando grew more and more irritable and jumpy.

I just was not happy with that young imp, not happy at all. . . .

When folk are immersed in animated conversations and the room fills with the racket, there often occur on this Earth unaccountable sudden silences. These occur at twenty minutes to or twenty minutes past the hour. In one such abrupt silence two things happened.

One—Twayne Gullik craftily snitched out his sword scabbard, tangled it in the busy legs of the little tump serving girl and toppled her over. The tray with its freight of half-empty wine cups spilled. Twayne Gullik laughed, a clever Ift scoring over a stupid tump in the eternal rivalry between the two races.

Murkizon snorted, and turned away, disgusted.

And, two—I said, hard edged to Pando: "Tell me, Kov Pando, why did you choose the zhantil as your emblem?"

He knew. Of course he knew, and he damned well knew I knew, too.

Pando gripped a gem-encrusted golden goblet. He looked down the table at me. "I recall a certain day, with the caravan, out in the New Territories of Turismond. I lost the pelt, seasons ago. But I said, then, and I kept my promise. The zhantil is the noblest wild animal—" He stopped himself, and then went on: "You called yourself Dray Prescot then."

"I have used the name, I admit," I said casually. "And the zhantil-masks we spoke of? I admire your craft there. It is a great gesture, potentially a jikai, to smash the leem-masks with zhantil-masks."

"And that is our true purpose!" cried Pompino, very bristly. "And not this unseemly wrangling among ourselves."

I hid my smile as I drank. My haughty Khibil comrade Pompino not enjoying a bout of wrangling! Come the day!

"Murgon has the king's ear," said Pando. He spoke moodily. "He is ensconced in the Zhantil Palace in Port Marsilus. He raises an army. I begin to think that perhaps he has won this bout, and maybe this is the last contest."

"Nonsense, kov!" said Pompino. "Do you not have the Vadni Dafni at your side!"

I must admit I wondered what the talkative Dafni would have to say about being lumped together as what

amounted to a chattel along with the king's ear and the
Zhantil Palace. Mind you, given the circumstances and
the customs, that was exactly the situation, and she was
enough of a noble lady to understand that. I wondered,
too, what she would do about it.

What she did do was to stand up and say—inter alia
with comments about the new dress she had ordered and
the way she required her eggs in the morning—that now
she would retire. Her handmaids went with her. Of all
the ladies left only one, I judged, might not wish to join
in the drinking and singing that would follow. Perhaps
two, if Pynsi Mytham was feeling too frail. The lady
Nalfi stood up. "I, too, will retire."

So that was a simple wager won.

Pynsi stayed on and this, I judged, was because Pando
did. We sang a few songs; but they did not rollick out
with the required gusto. We were not, all told, a happy
band.

In the end I'd had enough. I said to Dayra: "I'm for
bed."

So, Dayra, Pompino, two or three others, we made our
respects and cleared off to our quarters. Larghos vanished.
We slept. We awoke. We breakfasted. All that day we
argued back and forth, and Pando did not put in an
appearance. We renewed acquaintanceship with the
cadade, the captain of the guard, Framco the Tranzer. He
was pleased to see us, for he recognized the crew as
seasoned warriors. Naghan the Pellendur had copied his
cadade's habit of pulling his whiskers.

Everyone wanted to go and inspect the voller.

I said to Pompino, "We can't call her *Pride of Bormark.*"

"True. Well, let your young friend Pando sweat. We'll
call her *Golden Zhantil.*"

"Capital!"

At our own request we saddled up zorcas and rode
through the forests, admiring their richness. The animals were very fine, not as fine as Filbarrka's zorcas of
the Blue Mountains of Vallia, but then, as he would be
the first to say, there are no zorcas in all Kregen to
match his.

Three days thus passed in idleness and chatter.

On the fourth day we cantered back gently through
the falling shadows of indigo and bronze, looking forward
to a good meal. Pando had not put in an appearance, and

I was seriously considering going and trying to induce some sense into his thick vosk-skull of a head.

The longer we delayed, the greater Murgon's ambitions would rise, the greater his power extend.

We rode into the stockaded yard of the steading to find absolute chaos, stark raging madness.

When we'd shaken some sense into the nearest wight we could lay hands on he shook himself in fear. He was a Fristle guard, and he bore a great wound down his arm.

"Lords, lords! They came and took her away!"

"Who came? Took who?"

He shivered.

"I do not know who they were. They wore silver leem masks. And they took the Vadni Dafni away with them."

CHAPTER EIGHT

A roll of gold for
Jespar the Scundle

The first question to ask in these circumstances is: "Which way did they go?"

Murkizon growled out the question and the Fristle shook and shivered and stuttered: "Lord, lord, I do not know."

"Where's Pando?"

The uproar in the yard we now saw was mostly from slaves scared witless, men and women who had been wounded, and not a needleman in sight, and folk who just rushed about aimlessly. The kov, we learned, had ridden out in pursuit with a large party of his retainers and most of the guard led by the cadade.

"So he knew which way to go," said Pompino.

The hubbub continued unabated. Slaves were taking full advantage of the confusion to do what slaves tend to do given half the chance. I saw one fellow staggering off to the back quarters carrying an enormous jar—ale, probably—and followed by a raggle-taggle of his cronies. Other slaves were upsetting the side trestles, and roaring, and running. The bedlam battered on. We found a tump slave calmly sitting with his back against a wall stripping palines from a branch and popping them one by one into his mouth. He was happy. Well, not all tumps are your dour, taciturn, mining people who just dig in the ground for red gold and continually bicker with the Ifts of the forest—though tumps and Ifts bicker all the time, of course.

He wiped his mouth where the whiskers sprouted, for his beard reached to his belt, and swallowed the last morsel of paline and stood up.

"Masters, that Ift castellan, Twayne Gullik, led the pursuit."

From his manner, cowed and abject in the slave fashion though it was, you could tell what he thought of Ifts.

"So the kov did know which way to go." Pompino swung away energetically. "Well, that settles it." He drew me a little apart from our comrades, who were now intent upon finding their own suppers. "Jak, we have wasted too much time here shilly-shallying. We should be about the Star Lords' business, burning temples—"

"But this was part of the plan—"

"Assuredly. But burning temples to Lem the Silver Leem is by far the most important task we have at the moment. If your friendship for the kov Pando—whom I cannot profess to care overmuch for—prevents you from carrying out your duty to the Everoinye—"

I spoke hotly.

"I've told you, aye, and the Everoinye, what I think of their duty. They have caused me much anguish in the past. I know I distress you with these sentiments, Pompino; but they are sincerely held. The Star Lords plunk me down in unhealthy places and expect me to sort out their problems for them. All right. And I agree we must smash the Lemmites. But, right now, at this moment, I am concerned for Pando."

"Nobody knows which way he's gone!"

"True. But we can take the airboat and search."

He put his fists on his hips and glared at me, whiskers bristling, face flushed, foxy and brilliant and altogether a sharp customer.

"If I order my people to follow me, then—"

"Then I'll be on my own."

"And—you would?"

"Aye, Pompino, by the Black Chunkrah, I would!"

The moment blew up into the promise of a full-grown gale—and then the tump walked across. He was around four foot high, so he was well-grown and he looked up. "Masters?"

"Aye, what?" growled Pompino.

"That haughty Ift shouted out as they galloped off—"

"What?"

He shuffled from one splayed foot to the other. He screwed up that knobbly face with the long nose, squinting up at us.

I said, "I know how you tumps love to dig in the ground, and sing about your work, and bring forth ripe rich red gold. But if I gave you a gold piece, now, for your words, well—you are slave. What could you do with gold now?"

"I was not always slave, master, and I will not always be slave. There is a scheme. The red gold—"

"Your name?"

"Here they call me Jespar the Scundle, master."

I reached into my pouch, and my fingers felt the leather and the stitching and not much else—perhaps a dead moth—and I almost laughed.

"All our gold was melted or spent or fined away, Jespar the Scundle. Now, we must hurry. The kovneva will give you gold." I started off at a trot, and I yelled the old man-driving word I seldom use: *"Bratch!"*

Jespar the Scundle bratched.

Her handmaids were outraged and Naghan the Pellendur who had been left as a guard demurred. I brushed all that aside. Into Tilda's private apartments we went. I was after the loan of a gold piece; I need not have bothered.

Mindi the Mad stood beside the kovneva's bed. She wore her pale blue gown in that shadowy chamber of heavy drapes and mellow lamps and thick rugs. She lifted her head within the hood and I saw that pale, narrow, high-cheekboned face in the flesh for the first time. But, of course, I knew her well.

"You are the man they call Jak?"

I said: "A gold piece, Mindi. The tump here is entitled to his due. We must be after the kov and Dafni—"

"The kov is being misled—"

"Ha!" broke in Jespar, with a most unslavelike rasp of humor. "The haughty Ift Twayne Gullik is foresworn again!"

"Sink me!" I burst out. "If you knew Pando had gone the wrong way, why didn't you stop him?"

She did not flinch.

"I did not know then, for I have just scryed. And, anyway, they were out of the steading like a pack of wild leem."

A slushy, slurred and yet full voice from the bed said: "Is that . . . ?"

She sat propped against pillows, half in the shadow of a curtain draped from the bedhead. Her gross form mountained the bedclothes like The Stratemsk, across which monstrous mountains I'd ventured just before my first meeting with Tilda. She held out a hand. The cup slanted at an angle.

"Natalia! My cup is empty. If my cup is empty, you know—you know what—what will. . . ."

Her thick voice trailed off. A wisp of gossamer, the flash of a slender form, white arms tilting an amphora, and the kovneva Tilda's cup was once more full. She slopped some wine, drank some, stained the bedclothes a deeper pink, and said, "It is no use chasing after Pando. Or after Dafni. He will not—not find her. Let—let her go. No good will come of them. . . ."

She was, for this latter-day Tilda of the Many Veils, remarkably sober and lucid.

Of course, the suns had only just gone down. It was early in the evening yet.

A superb russet-clad form moved gently beside Pompino, and Dayra said: "Mindi the Mad. You can scry. Can you not tell kov Pando? And put us on the right path? You have the power, *I know.* . . ."

For a moment I held my breath. The Sisters of the Rose could produce girls whose command of sorcery ran deep, who were thaumaturges of a very high order. Delia had not taken her Witch's Vows. The SoR did not deign to call their girls with the magical powers sorceresses or witches, instead dubbing such a girl a vibushi. I glanced sideways at Dayra. Was she a vibushi, then, a mistress of the magical arts as well as of the Whip and Claw?

Mindi the Mad looked at Dayra.

"The kovneva has just expressed a wish that the lady Dafni be left to ride away—"

Pompino blew up then.

"That's it! By Horato the Potent! This is footling. Come on, let's leave this pestilential place and set about our proper business!"

By Krun! And wasn't that the temptation!

I said, "I believe our best ends will be served if we can prevent the union between Murgon and Dafni. As to any future marriage between Dafni and Pando, that is entirely a different matter."

"How serve our best ends?"

I couldn't tell Pando all of it. But, by Zair, I was in the frame of mind to cut through all this skullduggery. If Pompino knew the truth, he would change in his attitude to me, of course he would change. But then we might get things done quickly that now I had to beat about the bush to accomplish.

With her smooth voice modulated and level, Dayra said: "If this Murgon takes Dafni, he wins her province, that will make him even stronger with the king, and the temples you speak of will proliferate and flourish. . . ."

"All the more to burn!" grunted Pompino. But Dayra's words had made him think afresh.

He drew his dagger. Mindi flinched back and half raised her hand. No one really believed she could turn him into a little green toad. But the thought was there, stark in our minds.

Pompino presented the point of the dagger to Jespar the Scundle's throat. His left hand seized the long beard and jerked the tump forward and up.

"I am not a silly forest Ift, tump. I am a Khibil. Now you will tell me what I want to know."

Jespar strained on tiptoe. He remained calm.

"You may kill a slave, Khibil; you will not then learn what it is you wish to know."

Oh, yes, tough these tumps; tough as the rock they dig their red gold from.

I drew my knife; that broad heavy sailor blade caught a glint from the lamps and glittered. Jespar swiveled his eyeballs in my direction. I heard Dayra take a breath.

On the footrail of Tilda's bed, exposed by the drape of the clothes, the golden inlay gleamed lushly. The point of the knife slid in, I twisted, pulled, got the strip in my fingers and hauled. I was able to roll up a good arm's length of the golden inlay into a bundle. This I held out.

"You'd better put Jespar down, Pompino. You'll have that beautiful beard out by the roots else."

The Khibil laughed. He socked the tump back onto the soles of his feet, and said: "Well, tump? Tell us!"

Jespar the Scundle shook himself straight, grabbed the roll of the golden inlay, stuffed it away somewhere into his gray slave breechclout and drew the belt tight.

"Yes, Jespar," I said straightly. "Tell us it all." For I had not missed the inner significance of the tump's words.

"That haughty Ift, Twayne Gullik," he began. Then he realized just what I had said. He slid those deep eyes of his around to goggle at me again, and said in a rapid staccato: "The Ift shouted out Benorlad; but I knew the men in the silver leem masks had not come from there."

"Benorlad," jerked out Naghan, his Fristle whiskers quivering. "That's Murgon's damned great fortress in his stromnate of Ribenor—"

"Why, Jespar?" I said.

"Why—wasn't my second cousin's wife's brother there, with the men in the silver masks, with a chain around his neck and sitting on the back of a zorca? Tumps don't ride so grandly. And we don't like straying far. No, that wight Tangle the Ears—and I can't say I care for him over much for he got disgustingly drunk when my second cousin was married—was being made to act the guide. They're off to the mines up around the headwaters of the River Oonparl, up beyond Erronskorf."

I stared at Mindi the Mad.

"You knew this?"

She, in her turn, looked at Tilda. The gross form moved spasmodically as Tilda turned over, slopping wine, having had her say determined not to hear any more. Mindi took that as permission.

"Since you have discovered where Murgon is going, through chicanery—why, yes."

"Then," I said, swinging about and grasping Jespar, "do you scry and warn kov Pando. Tell him we are headed directly for Erronskorf. If he rides hard he may come up with us to be of use."

"But—" she began.

"You would be well-advised to do it," said Pompino. He spoke gravely. He meant what he said.

Jespar squealed in my grip.

"Lord, lord! I cannot ride a jut, let along aspire to straddling a zorca!"

"Oh," I said. "You won't have to worry about riding any animal the way we're going."

And, so, without more ado, off we trooped to gather our lads and to take after Strom Murgon and his silver leem masked rogues and the Vadni Dafni.

CHAPTER NINE

We drop in on Korfseyrie

Hurtling through the windrush under the Moons of Kregen we pelted headlong for Erronskorf.

Pompino gave orders for the crew to sleep by watches; I suppose some of us caught a few moments of sleep as we hurtled on in that streaming radiance from She of the Veils and the Maiden with the Many Smiles. One of the small moons bustled past above, swinging wildly through the star fields.

Because these Pandaheem were totally unacquainted with vollers, Dayra and I had to fly *Golden Zhantil* ourselves. Dayra proved a first-class pilot—well, by Zair! and didn't she ought to be, seeing her mother had taught her? Delia had also taught me my piloting. As for Delia, well, no doubt there were better pilots who flew vollers all day for a living, no doubt; my view remained exactly the same as the view which told me that Seg Segutorio was the best bowman of Kregen—Delia, likewise, was the best pilot in all the world. So said I.

Sitting quietly at the controls with the port-windows thrust wide I was privy to a vastly entertaining conversation between Rondas the Bold, our Rapa paktun, and the diminutive tump, Jespar the Scundle.

"Now, tump," said Rondas in his big blustery way, "you are very welcome to join our company. Why, we are fearsome and ferocious paktuns, aye, and at the moment we are serving without pay, seeing it was all fined away from us by a scoundrelly woman."

"I never thought to live to see the day mercenaries would serve without pay—"

Ronda's answering snort must have riffled his feathers splendidly. "No more did I, tump, by Rhapaporgolam the

Reiver of Souls! But, and listen good, we are in the habit
of going agio when we go into action—"

"Agio?" Jespar's voice was an alarmed squeak.

"Aye, dom, agio! You see, all of us put in our gold, into
the kitty, all of it. Then, when the battle's over we share
it out again."

"You mean, to keep it safe?"

"Fambly! No! Why, those who share it out are less
than those who put it in, onker! That way a fellow can
make a little on the side from a fight."

"I don't think—"

"It's all fair and above board. It's in every paktun
contract, I expect—anyways, it's in ours. So, you see,
tump, when we get to wherever this fight is to be, your
roll of gold will be in good hands."

"But . . . !"

I concentrated on flying the voller. By Krun! But they
were a rascally bunch, right enough.

The two girl varterists came up and when Jespar appealed to them, they gravely told him that as far as they
were concerned they went in for agio and—had they any
gold about them—it would have gone into the kitty along
with Jespar's roll of gold inlay.

"Why don't I just keep my own gold—?"

"What! And suppose you are killed!"

"Why, as to that," said Jespar, "I don't intend to get
into any fights!"

"Amazing!"

"Incredible!"

"Not believable," amplified Rondas. He must have
been mournfully shaking his great beaked head, very
vulturine, very menacing. "Coming with us and not getting into a fight!"

"I didn't want to come!" squeaked Jespar. "Anyway,
I'm just a guide. I wouldn't have come at all if that great
hulking apim fellow hadn't hauled me along—"

"Oh, you mean our Jak. Why, dom, you want to walk
very small when he's about. He'd as lief fry you up and
gulp you down as a tasty morsel between meals."

"I don't—" began the tump.

Alwim, very hard, said: "You'd better believe it."

"I do! I do!"

"Just as well," said Wilma, as hard as her sister.

With the light of two gorgeous Moons of Kregen in the

sky we deemed it not altogether opportune for a swift
and undetected onslaught. Below passed away forested
hills, very ghostly silver, most eerie in that streaming
light. Those we pursued would have ridden hard at the
beginning, and then have husbanded their mounts. We
could cover in a single bur the distance it would take
them to progress in ten or twelve.

This thought occurred to Pompino, for he walked up
and said, "I think we may reach this damned place before them." •

"That is likely. I hope so. The advantage will lie with
us, then."

"Only is this tump Jespar the Scundle speaks right."

"He speaks right, as far as he knows and guesses. If he
is wrong—"

"I'll chop his ears off!"

"It seems to me our little tump Jespar is in for a very
rough ride . . . ."

"Oh, he'll survive. Very tough, they are. And I'll tell
you something else. They're not as dull and stupid as the
Ifts make out. Both races tend to want to occupy the
same areas of forest, the Ifts for the trees and the tumps
for the gold under the ground. Why they don't go and
dig for gold somewhere else escapes me."

"Why should they? If the gold is in the ground, they'll
dig it out, and if a few trees are in the way—"

"The Ifts are mightily upset, by Horato the Potent!"

Because we took a circuitous route so as not to fly
directly over the hamlet of Erronskorf we took longer
than the flight strictly required. All the same, we were
very quickly there, and Dayra guided the voller down
into the shadow of the trees.

"And you are sure this is the path they must take?"
demanded Pompino.

"Aye, lord, this is the path." As we crowded out of the
voller under the stars and gazed around on the gently
swaying masses of trees, Jespar sounded confident. He
was back on his own stamping grounds. That perked him
up.

He pointed upward along the path between the tree-
clad slopes of the mountain.

"Up there lies the mine—more than one, belonging to
different branches of the family. Down there—" and the
jerk of his thumb was highly dismissive—"lies the forest

of the Ifts. This is the path they will follow to go up past
the mines to Korfseyrie."

I just hoped Jespar was right, as much for his ears as
anything. Murgon could hide Dafni away up here and no
one the wiser. Then he could strike where he willed.

He as good as held the provincial capital, Port Marsilus.
He was entrenched in the Zhantil Palace there. Now he
sought to erode further Pando's fast waning power.

Pompino's mind must have followed a similar train of
thought, for he growled out: "A pity that flat slug of a
King Nemo did not burn with his damned temple and
palace in Pomdermam. While he rules and supports
Murgon—"

"Murgon has a free hand here. Aye."

A pair of voices that were usually lovingly gentle broke
out in passionate argument in the shadows. We turned.

"Lisa! You are the most stubborn and willful of women!"

"And you are the most thick-headed and stubborn of
men!"

Pompino brushed up his whiskers. "I would not care to
step in to settle that," he observed, in a fine free way.

Quendur the Ripper quite clearly had not heard
Pompino's heartfelt remark. His face alive and working
with passion, Quendur stormed over to us. The golden
mask hanging from its straps in his fingers shook
violently.

"Horter Pompino! I appeal to you! Tell Lisa the Empoin
that as I love her I will not have her with me in this
fight! Tell, horter, spell out the recklessness of her folly!"

Pompino flung me such a look I had to turn away.

"Well, Quendur—you see—that is—" Pompino stamped
his foot. "By Horato the Potent! Am I to mollycoddle you,
Quendur, you, the great roarer of a pirate!"

"But—!"

"But nothing! If I tell Lisa not to join in the attack, do
you think she will listen?"

"We have kept her out of fights before."

"That was different."

Lisa walked up, quietly, contained, already fastening
the leather straps of her zhantil mask over her head.

"You see, my love. I am in the fight, and shall stand by
your side to keep you out of trouble."

"And may Pandrite aid me!"

"He will, he will." And Lisa the Empoin pulled the straps up tightly.

Larghos the Flatch pulled his bow from his shoulder and set about stringing it. He looked sullen. Then, looking up he said: "I could wish, Quendur, that the lady Nalfi shared the spirit of Lisa the Empoin."

At my side Dayra moved and was still. She was too much the great lady to say: "See? I told you so!"

"Rather, Larghos, you should praise your gods that the lady Nalfi does not foolishly run headlong into danger." Quendur swung his golden mask about dangerously in itself. "Where does she rest now?"

"She remained in the airboat. She said her foot pained her, and would bathe it in hot liniment."

Quendur grunted something unintelligible, and then this part of the preparations was over. Each one of us pulled on a golden zhantil mask provided from Pando's armory. Some were of brass, some steel with a wash of gilding. They did not restrict vision, and were light enough not to discommode a person in the heat of a fight. They might stop a blow across the face, although I was not too sanguine about that.

The two Moons, the Maiden with the Many Smiles and She of the Veils, slanted beyond the tree line and the Twins would be later this night. For a space a fragrant darkness englobed us in the perfumes of a Kregan nighted forest.

While there was little necessity to give orders to so cutthroat a band about how to lay an ambush, Pompino went along each side of the pathway, making sure the dispositions pleased him. We settled down to wait.

Well, we waited. When the Twins rose and the forest trail lit up in a fuzzy pink glory, I went over to Pompino, about to make a certain suggestion. He was holding Jespar by one ear.

"Now, Jespar, you have had us out here on a fool's errand! Confess! My blade is hungry for your ears!"

"No, lord, no! Master, my ear!"

I said, "You should know, Jespar the Scundle, that Horter Pompino can be very severe on villains' ears."

"That is sooth!" roared Pompino.

"You should be lucky your sobriquet is not Iarvin," I went on. "Had it been—" I sucked in my breath, and fell silent.

Pompino took the point. He let go of the tump's ear. "Now," he said in a more reasonable voice. "Where are they?"

"Perhaps they have been delayed, lord—lord, I am certain sure my second cousin's wife's brother would be used to guide them here. Otherwise, why did they have a chain about the neck of Tangle the Ears, and why mount him astride a zorca, where he was always in mortal peril of falling off?"

"Perhaps he fell off," I said.

"That great rast Murgon would stick him back and tie him on," quoth Pompino. And, that was true. . . .

"I'll have a look down the path a ways," I said.

"I'm with you," said Dayra.

"That will be enough!" snapped Pompino, quelling the instant desires of the rest to take a break from lurking in ambush. So, off down the trail went Dayra and I, looking to see what there was to see.

We found enough, and easily enough at that, to tell us what had happened.

Zorca hoofprints, many of them, in a milling marking of the ground. They had ridden up, and then they had halted, and then they had struck off through the forest and skirted our pretty little ambush.

When Pompino came down to see he was beside himself with rage and mortification. I realized I had to handle this situation—and especially Pompino the Iarvin—with fastidious care.

"They must have caught wind of us," said Pompino, when he could speak coherently.

"Highly unlikely, surely, with such a band as ours?"

"Aye, you are right. So—?"

"So let us not worry too much over that now. Jespar can lead us to Korfseyrie."

Pompino pulled his whiskers.

"An onslaught is different from an ambush."

"That is true. But we can use the voller—"

"The airboat? How?"

He'd taken off his golden zhantil mask and dangled it from his fingers. He was pretty livid with anger and frustration and primed to abandon the night's doings and return to Plaxing.

Dayra, also, removed her mask, as did I. The breeze

zephyred over my cheeks, and I felt pleased that shadows dropped down to conceal my face. Dayra spoke up briskly.

"Why, my dear Pompino, we all climb aboard, we sail over their heads, and we drop down on top of them."

"Ha!" Pompino swung his arms about. "That sounds a sure recipe for disaster, my lady—"

I said, "We believe from what Jespar and the others said there are between twenty and thirty of them. We either go now and drop on their heads, or we give in and go back."

"Who said anything about giving in?"

"This was the gist of your observations, surely?"

Pompino glared about truculently. He breathed hard. He scrubbed up his whiskers. As a kettle on the stove bubbles and boils before either being removed or blowing up, so the haughty Khibil bubbled and boiled.

"Very well. We drop on their heads. And if you are killed do not come whining to me with your head all a-dangling."

At his words I turned sharply and blundered back down the path. Dayra had suggested the stratagem, and she was coming with us, and if Quendur the Ripper thought he had problems with Lisa the Empoin, then he didn't know the half of it . . .

Delia and I had called our youngest daughter Velia, and we had done this out of love and grief and prideful memory of the older Velia, our second daughter. I did not wish to contemplate all the agonies that might follow on this night's doings.

There was enough of the night left in which, if we hurried, we could finish this affair.

Lisa said she was coming, and that was that, and the lady Nalfi expressed the perfectly natural desire not to be left alone in the forest. She looked flushed. It was decided she would stay in the cabin out of harm's way. We did not intend to make our call a long one.

Korfseyrie was well named.

During the day no doubt the korfs would wing about the high towers, darting specks of color in the suns shine as they sought their prey. Now they'd all be tucked up with heads under wings along the niches and crevices of the stone walls and towers. In the mingled lights of the Twins we slanted down.

The place was a solid fortress, buttressed against at-

tacks from the edge of the forest, its walls lofting sheer,
its towers dominating every access. Being built in
Pandahem no thought had been given to attack from the
air.

"How well d'you know the place?" demanded Pompino.

Jespar whiffled and evaded; but in the end he admitted
that he had a passing acquaintance with the fortress.

"How passing?"

"We-ell. . . ."

"Spit it out!"

The place spread below, coming up fast, a confusing
medley of lights and shadows. Dayra flew the voller in a
tight circle aiming to land us on a flat-roofed construction high in the center. The flatness glimmered pink.
Each corner of the roof supported a squat tower.

Jespar looked over the sides as Pompino's groping fingers sought his ear.

"If you land there you'll get wet!"

"A damned rooftop reservoir!" said Pompino. "Catches
the rain. My lady Ros, we must find another—there!
That courtyard looks promising."

Dayra said nothing but flicked the flier into a tight
turn, scraped past the edge of a corner tower and brought
her to ground in a superb display of flying which was
completely wasted on these Pandaheem to whom the
vollers were simply magical and to be expected to do
magical things.

The moment I'd clapped eyes on this place I'd regretted
my suggestion of attacking it.

So maybe it was not planned to defeat an onslaught
from the air, so maybe the sentries were singlemindedly
watching for our approach up the narrow and tortuous
path to the summit, so what. . . . We were down in a yard
high in the complex, Jespar could show us the way; but
we were dreadfully few to accomplish a mission against a
stronghold and its garrison as strong as Korfseyrie.

Pompino had secured enough directions from Jespar to
take us through to Murgon's quarters. We didn't then
discover just what were the passing acquaintanceships
the tump had with this fortress; but Jespar was perfectly
confident in his directions. Soundlessly we leaped over
the bulwarks of the flier and raced into the shadows.

CHAPTER TEN

Jak Leemsjid

We reached the first shadowed doorway unobserved and I paused and looked back at the airboat.

If a satisfied grimace cracked my battered old features into a gargoyle smile, I was not only allowed that, and deserved it, by Vox, I joyed in it!

From the bulwarks Dayra stared after us. She saw me stop and look back, and she shook her fist at me.

She had said, very hot, very intemperate: "Why should *you* go and *I* stay?"

"Because you can fly the voller—"

"I believe you have some small skill in flying, Jak the Onker!"

"That is beside the point—"

"Or is it that you think me not a ferocious enough fighter to go?"

"If ferocity were all, then you would outdo all of us—"

"Then it is my skill and prowess at arms that disqualifies me in your sight?"

"Not at all, your skill—"

"Well, then, what?"

Pompino and Murkizon and Quendur and the rest looked on and took their own enjoyment from the scene and my predicament. I couldn't burst out: "Because you are my daughter, Dayra, that's why! And I'm not having you uselessly killed like Velia!"

I did say in my churlish way: "By the disgusting diseased liver and lights of Makki Grodno, girl! You'll stay with the guard and fly the voller out if you're attacked and you can hang about and fly down to pick us up when we get out!"

She opened her mouth—and I looked at her, and Dayra or no damned Ros the Claw, she shut up.

I admit to no proud feelings in this, on the contrary, to my discomfiture; but I knew what was what and Dayra was the pilot among us to stay in the voller.

Queyd-arn-tung!

There is no more to be said!

As we took breath in the shadowed doorway a second figure appeared beside that of Dayra at the bulwarks.

A fierce raspy voice said in my ear: "I give you thanks, Jak, that you made Ros Delphor see sense, for Lisa the Empoin was constrained to obey me—for a change." I said, "They'll be up to mischief, don't fear, Quendur."

"I know. I do not wish to contemplate that—"

"In here and stop lollygagging!" rapped Pompino.

Dutifully, we all went into the first of the chambers and looked about, our weapons ready, our senses alert.

Jespar mumbled: "I should have stayed, too. You know the way—"

"Think of your ear," said Pompino, "and lead on!"

Korfseyrie was large enough to require a sizable garrison and it was highly unlikely that the twenty or thirty with Murgon would spread out. When we bumped into one, we'd find most of them, or so we reasoned. The place smelled of damp and decay and bore an abandoned feeling, for Pando seldom ever came here and the place, designed to guard the mines worked by the tumps as well as the forests below, had been bypassed in the late wars. Murgon had shown craftiness in selecting it as his temporary headquarters.

We passed a tall window from which the glass had long since fallen. The stars glittered through the opening and a zephyr stole in and rippled the tapestries on the wall opposite.

Instantly, the movement at his side registered in the corner of his eye, Rondas struck.

The tapestry split. Dust puffed out chokingly. The whole tapestry simply ripped and fell into pieces, whole soft swaths of it disintegrating and collapsing across the corridor.

Nobody passed a comment.

A mail-armored and axe-armed man could have been waiting behind the arras, ready to leap out and decapitate one of us as his comrades roared into the fray.

Those decrepit tapestries were symbolic of the whole

fortress. Decrepit, dusty, disintegrating. Just how old it was we didn't care to guess; it was old. . . .

However unwilling and complaining he might be, Jespar led us in what I considered to be a reasonably straight line through the corridors and chambers. For all Pompino's tough manner, and the paktuns' casual menace when they suggested agio, we all felt affection for the little tump and the fearful threats made were merely that, threats and not to be acted upon. At least, I trusted that was so. . . .

Cautiously we descended from that high courtyard going down broad staircases and narrow spiral staircases, prowling along corridors darkened by shredded tapestries and drapes. No statuesque harnesses of armor, no stands of weapons arranged in decorative patterns, adorned the walls. They had all long since been taken away to be used in the red tumult of battle. Weapons and armor must serve many seasons when the wars are on.

Now the castle-builders of Kregen do not usually construct their fortresses so that any raggle-taggle-bobtail crew may calmly stroll in as though out for a Sunday promenade. They set traps. They confuse by winding stairways and corridors. They trick the unwary in a myriad of cunning, ingenious and lethal stratagems.

If you are unable to garrison the whole of your fortress, then you seal off those parts undefended and set the traps. We had the great advantage that we descended from the upper levels instead of fighting our way in over the ramparts as any sensible Pandaheem besieger would have to do. Jespar was aware of many of the places where we would have been slain for sure, and our own expertise took care of most of the rest.

Most of the rest. . . .

"There are murdering holes in that ceiling," pointed out Rondas the Bold, "and arrow slits in the walls."

"Aye," agreed Pompino. "Where is the trigger?"

Jespar professed himself at a loss.

"This must have been set up after Kov Pando left."

"Well," I said, venturing an opinion, "if no one has been here much since, this could be Murgon's work, therefore we look for places where the dust does not lie as thickly—as there!"

The plate in the floor was suspiciously free of the dust

that clung stubbornly everywhere. We could mark our
route in the dust of the floors.

"You could be right."

"We shall see," said Rondas, and he took off his heavy
helmet, swung it by the straps, and hurled it full onto
the plate. The metal rang gonglike.

Instantly, the nearest murdering holes disgorged a fuming liquid that stank in the confines of the corridor, and
the nearest arrow slits ejected barbed darts that flew to
smash rendingly against the opposite walls.

Bold as ever, Rondas laughed, and stepped forward to
retrieve his helmet, no doubt concerned lest the feathers
were damaged.

"Wait!" screeched Pompino.

Rondas took two steps more and bent, and the whizz of
the dart passed just over his head. From the murdering
holes more fuming liquid poured, stifling us in the stench.
Rondas let out a yell, and leaped back, half-straightening
as he jumped. The second dart took him full in the back.
It punched through his carelessly flung cape, and as he
reeled under the blow I leaped, grabbed him, hauled him
in like a fisherman reeling in his catch. Rondas fell all of
a heap.

We staggered back.

Rondas said, "May all the devils of Gundarlo take
it—my back, horters, my back!"

We turned him onto his front so that his great beak
jutted to the side and lifted the cape away. The barb had
dinted into his armor, breaking a way through. Dark
blood welled.

Pompino pursed up his lips.

"It is deep; but not so deep as to be fatal, as I judge.
You have been lucky, my Bold friend."

"Lucky! My back feels it has been broken in two!"

"Well, the dart must be got out, and that is a job for a
needleman, of whom we have none. So—"

"I can make it back to the flying boat," gasped Rondas.
"Even if I crawl. Do you go on."

I said, "I am not prepared to see Rondas die for lack of
attention—"

"What do you suggest, then, Jak? Abandon our rescue?"

"If necessary. The Vadni Dafni can always be rescued
another time—this whole venture is—"

"I know! It is foolhardy, harebrained and stupid! But

we are in for it now, mostly thanks to you. So I shall go
on, by Horato the Potent!"

"Very well."

He glared at me, very huffy, very arrogant, brushing
up those reddish whiskers into a bristling stiffness.

"If that is your desire, Jak the—Jak the—"

"Call me Jak the Onker, and it would fit. We cannot go
on through that corridor, I judge—"

"That is right, master!" broke in Jespar, babbling in
his eagerness. "The traps are fresh and strewn thickly."

"So you will have to find another way through, Pompino
the Iarvin."

Cap'n Murkizon, who appeared somewhat at a loss
because of the absence of Larghos the Flatch on guard by
the voller, banged his axe about, mentioning his Divine
Lady, and suggesting we stop blathering and get on with
it. I believe he had missed a deal of the byplay, the words
not spoken, between Pompino and me.

Now Pompino cast about and spotted a secondary
corridor. He pointed that way, nose in the air, filled with
a quivering fury.

"Let us go, then, by Horato the Potent!"

The way led for a time back the way we had come and
if Pompino noticed this he did not comment thereon. I
supported Rondas, fairly hauling him along, concerned
at the state he was in. Arrow and dart wounds are the
very devil if they are not treated correctly. I judged that
the barb although not overly deep was deep enough to
present problems. It could not be pushed all the way
through, as a slender arrow might with a smart blow,
mainly because it was aimed directly into the vitals of
the Rapa. It would have to be cut out. This I could do,
and had done aforetimes; it was not something I was
overly fond of having to do. Also, to weigh the balances
in our favor, Rondas was a tough bullyboy of a fellow,
able to stand the shock of my rude ministrations. He
would not keel over like others might have done who had
previously caused Seg and me some headaches.

The Fristle guard commander, Naghan the Pellendur,
told off one of his men to assist me, and between us we
carried Rondas along more comfortably.

As we went along I decided that I didn't care what
Pompino might do. He was my comrade and we both
worked for the Star Lords. If he wished to continue the

rescue attempt then he would do so and I would not seek
to prevent him. I did know that I was taking Rondas
back to the voller where I'd put out my utmost exertions
to see that he did not die from his wound.

The others pressed on and Naghan half-turned.

"Maybe it would be safer if a couple of us went with
you, horter Jak."

"My thanks, Naghan; but with Nath the Gristle here
to help, we should manage."

The Fristle guard assisting me made no comment.

The Pellendur nodded, satisfied, and swung off after
the main party. We'd reached a bend in the corridor
where the Twins shafted their light, still eerily tinged
with a ghostly silver glow, across the walls, covered in
faded paintings, from an arched opening above.

Dust motes spun in the still air. The men ahead seemed
phantoms, specter figures moving in moonbeams and
magic. The whole wall at our side collapsed and fell
away on hidden hinges. A pit gaped beside us.

The Fristle guard, Nath the Gristle, and Rondas would
have fallen, tottering off balance. I managed to give
them both a fierce twisting shove, a gasped effort like
the release of a spring. They toppled away from the pit.

Then, in the same instant, I was falling, spinning head
over heels through thin air.

A frenzied hullabaloo started above, a chorus of shocked
yells and oaths. The sounds racketed between the stone
walls. I hit with an almighty thump, thwacking down
flat on my back onto a heaping pile of filthy straw.
Mangy bits of straw fluffed, the stink was immense, and
all the stars of Kregen flashed before my eyes and the
cacophony of the Bells of Beng Kishi clamored in my
skull.

"You all right, Jak?"

Pompino's shout was an echo, floating around in
darkness, an alarmed yell of despair.

I couldn't—for the moment—answer.

"Jak!"

I drew in a breath that nigh gagged me.

"You'll wake up the whole damn fortress. . . ."

"Thank Pandrite—we'll soon have you out."

A hiss, a particular venomous malevolent hiss, drew
my shocked attention. I came quiveringly alert. I knew,

at once and without a doubt, what kind of creature stalked me from the shadows.

Up above on the lip of the pit, out of jumping distance, my comrades crowded to peer down. They saw. They saw the lean slinking form lope out into the shafts of moonlight.

That lethal shape halted when the first shaft of moonlight struck down. In that pallid radiance the eyes gleamed, gleamed—oh, how those eyes gleamed!

The wedge-shaped head sank down, low to the stone, and the mouth gaped wide revealing rows of yellow teeth and the purple-black gums, from which spittle-foam dribbled down. Slavering, those jaws opened wide.

Delicately, step by step, two feet at a time, one from each side, the eight clawed feet lifted and fell and the long lean body bore down on me. The tail flicked from side to side, sinuous, quivering, and the tip was truly tufted by a clot of black hair. The muscles stirred the furred pelt, long iron-hard muscles, moving with smooth precision under the ocher hide. Low to the ground, head out-thrust, two feet after two feet, tail flicking, death stalked me in that moonlight-drenched pit.

One of the Fristle guards hurled his spear and thankfully he missed the leem.

More usefully, Nath Kemchug shouted: "Hai!" and threw down his spear to me. It clattered on the stones and the butt end rested on the pile of stinking straw by my foot.

At the Chulik's shout the leem paused and his wicked head with the whiskers stiff as steel spikes tilted up. I reached out a slow, steady, cautious hand for the spear.

My fingertips touched the iron-bound wooden butt; and then froze. The leem snarled at me, ignoring the people up above who were all now shouting and screaming trying to draw the beast's attention.

Two more spears flew.

"Belay that!" I yelled, risking an immediate attack. "You might hit him!"

No more spears hurled down.

Two clawed feet at a time, eight feet lifting and putting down, the leem moved from the shadows into the light of the Twins. His two shadows lay close together, so for a bewildering moment it seemed there were three leems stalking me in the pit. . . .

My fingers wrapped around the iron-shod butt. Nath

Kemchug was proud of his spear. It was stout and sturdy, with plenty of steel weighted in the head. He could polish up his tusks a treat with it.

The saliva glimmering on the teeth of the leem dripped down from those purple-bruised gums. His tail flicked from side to side—was he one of the sort who straightened his tail into a bar in the instant he charged? Or was he of that diabolical sort who waggled his damned tail even when he leaped? I did not know. My fingers eased up the smooth wooden haft of the spear, and I was at full stretch, and knew that if I moved too much too quickly the bolt of ocher-furred lightning would strike. . . .

Sensations fined down. I could feel the polished wood as rough as sandpaper. The stink wafted away and became as nothing, the dung-heap stench vanishing and instead my nostrils filled with the smell of leem. I could see the way his whiskers indented, each in its own little black pit. I could see the sparkle of each drop of spittle. I could see the angry-red tongue, lolling behind those fangs. His ears lay close to his head, swiveled to catch the first sound of an enemy elsewhere than where he knew he had his prey firmly fixed. And his eyes! Partially veiled by a downdroop of brow, semicircles of hate, the eyeballs turned up so that the eye looked a blot of mirror darkness cupped in a rind of yellow-white, those eyes fastened on me with such merciless determination I knew that I'd have one heartbeat and one only to save myself.

As that thought shot through my head I realized I was glad Dayra was not up there, crowding to the lip of the pit with the others.

I do not know how long the interval was between my falling into the pit and the instant the leem charged. It could not have been very long. Leems are sudden beasts in their ferocity; to me that time passed in an agony of slowness. It seemed a long time to me, a damned long time.

Then I had the spear in my fists, had thrust the butt into the crack of stone just beyond the pile of straw and the leem was in midair above me, his paws widely extended, his mouth a single vast cavern. . . .

One way and one way only to go—

Headlong I dived under him, between the rows of taloned paws. His belly shot past above and the steel spear point penetrated his breast and went on and on and he

went on also. Had I stayed another heartbeat, he would
have landed full on me. The spear passed completely
through him, jutting up a reeking and gory splinter
above his back.

His screeching scream shattered against the walls of
the pit and echoed crazily in my head.

I was on hands and knees, was turning, seeing his
tufted tail quivering before my face. He thrashed and
screamed and pawed at the spear, and blood sprayed.

He wasn't dead. Not by a long long way do you kill a
leem by merely passing a spear through his body. Even if
you hit one of his hearts, the other will pump fresh anger
and power into his muscles.

If my comrades were yelling, I could not say. If the
world had blown up, I didn't know. The noise in my head,
compounded of the leem and my own blood, drowned out
sanity. My thraxter was in my fist. What a weapon to
fight a leem! I leaped to the side, skidding, and he turned
and tried to leap again and this time I was poised and
ready. The thraxter went in neatly and I swear the last
foot of the blow was in midair, for I was already turning
and leaping away and snatching up one of the Fristles'
flung spears.

Give a leem no chance—he never gives anyone or anything a single chance in all of Kregen—give him no
rest. . . . The first spear, muscled by desperation, flew to
embed itself in his flank and bit, as he swiveled to leap
again. He did not move as fast as he had. . . . His blood
choked upon the floor and fouled among the foulness of
the straw. . . .

Flashing the second spear before his face, shooting a
jagged reflection of moons shine into his eyes, checked
him for a tiny moment. He was a fine specimen, powerful,
savage, a killing machine. I believe the spear in his
flank must have nicked his secondary heart; for as he
swiveled and prepared to leap again he was slow. I poised
the spear. I drew a breath, realizing that that simple act
meant I was back in control of myself and was a fighting
intelligence rather than a mere primordial warrior-savage.
His tufted tail lashed. His eyes fastened on me like
leeches. His scarlet cavern of a mouth gaped and the
yellow fangs glittered with saliva. Blood pumped from
his side.

In the next instant he would leap . . .

So, mastering myself, remembering I was Dray Prescot, Lord of Strombor and Krozair of Zy, I bellowed out: "Hai!" and charged in full tilt.

Savage against savage, beast against beast . . .

The cruel steel spear head drove deeply into the ocher beast's breast as the apim beast that was myself forced on the shaft with bursting muscles.

Almost, he had me then.

A paw swiped from nowhere and even as I ducked a claw razored down my cheek. Had he connected full that blow would have split my head as an axe splits kindling, a child squashes a rotten fruit.

Hanging onto the spear I twisted, grinding it in, shouting, redness and haziness everywhere.

Someone shouted: "Hai!"

Pompino was there, before me, a spear in his fists driving down.

I said, "Thank you, Pompino—"

He said, "It was fast, too fast—my help was not necessary."

Staggering back, feeling the wetness of my own blood on my face, I gulped air. The stench was prodigious. The leem lay on his side, eyes rolled up, a last long shaky quiver trembling his lean flank. The dark tufted tail gave a last twitch.

"Hai!" bellowed down Murkizon.

The others set up a yelling. I sat down, plump, on the blood-soaked straw.

Probably the perfectly natural reaction of a fellow after a fight overwhelmed me then. Normally I can contrive to carry on with some at least of the old functions still operative after combat. But, for some reason, on that occasion, with the dead leem and the blood and the stink—and the very real horror coiled in me at thought of what might have occurred had Dayra been with us when I fell into the pit—I babbled like a green young coy after his first brush with the foe.

"A leem!" Quendur said, leaping down and giving the dead carcass a kick. "That is a jikai—a lone man—"

So, loose-tongued, chattering, I said: "A leem? But I had a sword, and spears, so I had all the advantages. I've fought leems before. Once, I recall, I fought a leem with a kutcherer, that silly butcher knife with the spike at the back. That was a bad one. He chewed me up; but I got him in the end. Leems, no, doms, I do not like leems and have fought them many times, and each time I swear will be the last."

"You speak strangely, Jak." Pompino turned his head to stare at me instead of the leem. The furred, feline and vicious fighting cat lay there in his own blood, and he looked pathetic now, as so many dead creatures do. . . .

"Strangely?"

"Aye. A lone man against a leem no matter what his weapons and skill is a jikai not lightly to be undertaken. Even professional leem-hunters, who are all mad anyway, do not operate alone. You were a leem-hunter?"

"Not a professional—I only fight leems when I have to. . . ." And, as you know, that was not strictly true. . . .

"A jikai," boomed Murkizon. "That is what I call this deed and that is what it is, a jikai. Hai, Jak Leemsjid!"

Jak Leemsjid. . . .

They all took up the cry.

So, I had acquired a sobriquet, at last, after my simple name of Jak.

Leemsjid, leemsbane. . . .

I said, "If that is so, we must prove myself equal to the name. The Leem Lovers—"

"Aye!"

I stood up. I retrieved the thraxter. I cut off that dark tuft at the tip of the leem's tail. This I tucked down into my harness. Then we were hauled out of the pit and so set off again, and now Rondas the Bold was assisted along by a rascally savage fellow rejoicing under the new name of Jak Leemsjid.

CHAPTER ELEVEN

We assist at Strom Murgon's feast

The way before us was blocked solidly by a mass of masonry extending from wall to wall and from floor to ceiling.

"The devil take it!" exclaimed Pompino.

He twisted up Jespar's ear.

"Well, tump!"

"I do not know, master! Maybe, maybe the noise—we were heard—maybe Murgon has triggered more traps—"

"That cross-passage fifty paces back may lead us in the direction we wish to go," suggested Naghan the Pellendur. He glanced at the slumped figure of Rondas the Bold. "We must hurry—"

"Aye," said Nath Kemchug, busy with rags and oil.

I took great heart from this small exchange. I have said many times that most of the folk of Kregen did not get on with Rapas. But one became accustomed to their smell after a time. Not all were evil. No more than any other of the races of Kregen—excepting Katakis and some others, who were damned of the devil and doomed in all men's eyes.

Now a Chulik and a Fristle were concerned for the life of a Rapa.

As I say, that heartened me.

We retraced our steps in the dust to the cross-passage and ventured along it in semi-darkness.

Pompino said to me: "I suppose that damned great gash in your face will heal up with uncanny speed, as always?"

I grunted something. Pompino was not aware that I'd bathed in the Sacred Pool of Baptism in far Aphrasöe and this gave me seemingly miraculous healing abilities. There was so much Pompino did not know of me, and I was his comrade, a fellow kregoinye. Well, the dark glass holds the future, as they say. Now, as we shuffled on through the dusty corridors, I felt the weight of Kregen pressing down on me.

The walls and ceiling floated echoes down oddly from up ahead. Pompino and Jespar were yammering away, and although they spoke in fierce staccato whispers, the sounds bounced off the stone and reached us at the tail. They might, also, reach other ears, set each side of heads filled with plots for our destruction. There was no doubt we had made a lot of noise. Now ordinary noise in a castle can fade and attenuate from one ward to another, muffled by thick walls and lost. A fight can bring the guards arunning, as all of us here knew. That damned leem . . . He must have been a precious part of the Leem Lover's paraphernalia, for the slinking lean forms of leems are not easily come by—alive in good condition.

So, we expected company at any moment.

Nath Kemchug's ministrations on his spear were almost finished. He carried oil flask and rags like any warrior to keep his armory clean, and again like any warrior wasn't too choosy whose wall he knocked over to get some brick dust. Of spittle we usually had a plentiful supply, except when our mouths dried in the fear and clangor of combat, and then we were not particularly thinking about cleaning blood off our weapons—quite the reverse.

But with Pompino's mercenary Chulik the cleaning of spear took precedence over all of his other weaponry. There was obsession in this. Chuliks, trained from birth to handle any weapons, continue to perplex and baffle me, and while they could handle—and clean—any weapon, Nath Kemchug remained obsessed with his spear. As we were making so much noise, I did not hesitate to call across to him over Rondas's drooping shoulder.

"I give you thanks, Nath Kemchug, for the use of your spear. The weapon served well."

He was down at the butt end, meticulously picking away at the junction of wood and iron, removing all traces of the leem's blood. He did not look up as he spoke in his apparently surly Chulik way.

"You fought well. In the name of Father Chalkush of the Iron Brand, I give you the jikai for that, Jak Leemsjid."

Rondas, sagging in my grip, let out a gurgling groan of

a laugh at that. Surly, Chuliks appear to the world; I was beginning to believe that my original estimate of them, founded as it was upon ignorance and prejudice, might be more in need of rethinking than I supposed. And, the same estimate applied to Rapas, and to Fristles. Truly, the more I spent my life on Kregen and learned of the ways of that ferocious and mysterious world, the more I understood how little I really knew!

Men are men and women are women, and that is the beginning and end of the mystery.

Pompino's voice floated up. He sounded absolutely revolted at what he had just heard. He sounded disgusted.

"What, tump! Down *there!*"

"Aye, master. It seems to be the only way through."

Another of those uncannily appearing blocks of masonry walled off the passageway ahead. If we went back we'd only run into the other block, or be forced to try the passage where Rondas took his wound. At the side of the block the dark round opening of a hole promised fearful terrors. The smell was bad enough; there was no leem stink mixed with it as far as we could sniff.

"By Horato the Potent! This expedition is not turning out as I expected!"

"Strom Murgon is a very clever man, master—"

Pompino turned to look down, and he turned and looked very slowly and with great meaning. Now by this time we'd all taken off our zhantil masks—if I'd been wearing mine when I fought the leem I wondered how little protection it would have afforded my face against those horrific claws—so that Pompino's haughty Khibil face could fully express the depth of his feelings. He stared at the little tump.

"And are you then suggesting that I am not?"

Jespar quaked.

"No, master! Of course not—"

For a reason not at all obscure I said: "Jespar is too wise in the ways of this world to make elementary mistakes, apart from being made slave and then of going with us. I think he should be listened to—"

"But, Jak, down there!"

Cap'n Murkizon boomed out: "Show us another way, horter Pompino, and we will gladly follow it."

There being no answer to that, we all dropped down

the black hole into the stink, one after the other. And, of course, Pompino dropped down first.

We managed to bring Rondas down without causing him overmuch pain. His mail had saved his life. But if we did not get the barb out within a reasonable time, and patch him up, he could easily lose that precious commodity.

Jespar's squeak said: "We are approaching Murgon's quarters. I am sure of it."

Nobody could see a blind thing. We shuffled along a narrow ankle-breaking slit in which muddy water ran. If this was a drain and someone pulled the plug up aloft, well, we'd be neck high, or mouth high, in filthy water—or drowned.

I made up my mind I'd see to it that Jespar was lifted up so that he stood the same chance as folk of races not dumpy and near to the ground.

We came to a fork where our hands met emptiness each side.

"Which way, Jespar?" growled Pompino.

"To—to the right, master, lies Murgon's suite—I think."

"And to the left?"

"I am not sure. If this drain lies under the Corridor of Fountains, then the left would lead to the drain opening onto the cliff—"

"To the right, then."

A moment's thought assured me that to emerge onto the cliff, separated from Dayra and the voller by the bulk of the fortress, would not serve my purpose. We had to go back and up. If that way lay through Murgon's apartments, then that was the way we would have to go.

When we came across a ladder Pompino halted.

"I am going up. I am heartily sick of this drain."

Perforce, up we went. When Nath the Gristle and I maneuvered Rondas up onto the paving through the man-hole we found ourselves in a narrow space walled by masonry and brick. Lanternlight fell through a lattice-work a score of paces off to our right. That was the way Pompino led.

Now we padded along silently, feral, alert, and with weapons in our fists.

The sound of voices reached us, and at this we all took heart.

Soundlessly, we approached the latticework and peered through.

Had an observer chanced to spy us he must have jumped back, aghast. At the best of times an unruly, fearsome, hairy bunch, after our experiences with Murgon's traps, our struggles in the corridors and pits, and to top it off the trudge through the slimy stink of the drain, we must now appear a truly awful, horrendous bunch of scarecrows.

Pompino put his nose against the stone latticework. He sniffed. That sharp cunning foxy nose wrinkled, and he sniffed again.

About to make a tart comment that we were aware that we all stank, I stopped. I, too, sniffed.

"Undoubtedly," pronounced Pompino.

Cap'n Murkizon said with enormous satisfaction: "Roast vosk for a certainty."

"And momolams."

We were all sniffing away at the delectable odors drifting in through the latticework. Our own stinks were forgotten.

Everyone smelled out his favorite dish. They were all there.

"If this is not another trap . . ." said Pompino.

"It's got to be Murgon's kitchens."

"True. But I have the deepest suspicions of anything that man does. None of you will rush upon the viands. If you do—"

Rather tartly, I reminded them.

"I do not believe Rondas the Bold will go rushing anywhere for a time."

That was cruel of me, of course; for they were all aware of Rondas' plight; but I felt the responsibility in an odd way. As the others led off, going cautiously, and Nath the Gristle and I followed on with Rondas between us, I reflected that I'd taken enough responsibility in my life, Zair knew, and taken it damned ungraciously usually. Responsibility to others, to some shadowy creed, to your own damned stupid self, sometimes weighs a fellow down more heavily than all the iron shackles in Kregen.

When we fetched up with the others in a vaulted barnlike place with two walls roaring with fireplaces, with broad tables groaning with provender, with pots abubbling and pans afrying and spits aroasting, the glorious mouth-watering scents of any gourmet's paradise enclosed us in a world of enchantment.

The cooks and serving folk huddled against the one wall that held only shelves, and a posse of Naghan's Fristles prodded absently at them with their spears one-handed, while they gorged on whatever came to the other hand.

Nothing loath, for like them all we were sharp-set, Nath the Gristle and I plunged for the nearest food-piled table. Rondas, comfortably on his side, appeared not the least interested in food. We took him back a drink, which eased his thirst but was probably not too clever, although I was confident the dart had not penetrated into his intestines.

Pompino rolled over, swallowed down, hiccoughed, and said: "Murgon is in the middle of a feast. I imagine he will not wait too long for the next course."

"He won't tolerate slack service." I spoke solemnly, already gleeing at what was to follow.

For, of course, Pompino the Iarvin as a smart kregoinye, saw as fast as did I—probably faster—what the next ploy would have to be.

"Although, Pompino, I also won't tolerate delay in attending to Rondas."

"There's a needlewoman at the feast. I asked."

"Then I am with you and let us try to knock some sense into these rascals of ours. . . . They'll stuff themselves silly given half a chance."

With superb food distending their stomachs, their blood still hot from the insults they had received within this place, the lads were very much inclined to go and do nasties to Strom Murgon and his cronies. An eye for an eye, reprehensible though that may be, tended to operate at certain levels.

I said to Pompino: "Mind you, Murgon is feasting late. The night won't last forever. One wonders what was the occasion, apart from the lady Dafni, of course."

"A fellow doesn't really need an excuse for a feast, Jak Leemsjid!"

I agreed. As Pompino spoke the new name, I realized that there was a certain lack, a wanting of euphony. The name needed a lightening syllable. . . .

In no time at all once the idea had taken hold on their evil imaginations, the crew and the guards dressed in

the flamboyant if shoddy festive robes of the servitors.
They disguised themselves amid much stifled laughter.
Weapons were hidden. Quendur stuffed his sword into an
enormous pie, and swathed a yellow hot-serving cloth
about the hilt, guffawing.

Soon, choking to keep down their merriment, their
weapons hidden and ready, their festive serving garments,
all swathing multi-colored cloths and feathers and baubles,
disguising the grimy bodies beneath, they were mar-
shaled into a procession. Trays bearing a bewildering
assortment of foods for the next course hoisted high to
conceal their faces, they marched solemnly for the doorway leading into the banqueting hall.

I, Dray Prescot, walked with them, clad as were they,
my weapons hidden as were theirs.

We were going to serve up Strom Murgon with an
unexpected delicacy.

Every one of us wore a golden zhantil mask.

And, with us, clinging like a vile miasma, the stink of
our passage through the sewers floated about us.

So, dressed up, kitted up, with sharp weapons, stinking to high heaven, we entered Strom Murgon's banqueting hall.

CHAPTER TWELVE

Golden zhantil-masks

"Bratch, you rasts, bratch!" called a silly foppishly dressed fellow who must be the overseer of the servers. We ignored him. We marched on in stately procession, carrying the viands high to conceal the golden zhantil-masks.

Strom Murgon sat in state in this banqueting hall of Korfseyrie. The chamber bore none of the marks of long disuse of the other parts of the fortress. Tapestries glowed upon the stone walls. The beams above were carved and gilded. The tables in the form of a horseshoe carried fine yellow napery, and silver and gold vessels, and banked vases of flowers. Incense hung in the air, which stank worse than we did from the sewers. Murgon's cronies sat about the tables, facing inward to the hollow center. Among them lolled many painted girls in transparent draperies.

In the space between the arms of the horseshoe tables a troupe of erotic contortionists performed. This explained the lack of urgency in chasing up the next course of the feast. They'd been sitting here enjoying themselves since they'd avoided us in the forest and settled down to a night of debauchery and they were not halfway through yet.

The orchestra in a grilled enclosure to one side donged and plucked and tootled away. The performing troupe performed. There were Sylvies there—as one expected—and they always gave within the expertise of their art superlative exhibitions.

From a bulky grotesquely clothed form with a silver tray bearing a whole roasted bird stuffed with smaller birds ad infinitum a throaty rumble said: ". . . .Belschutz!"

"Such decadence is to be expected," whispered Pompino.

"But there are still guards lining the walls."

"Oh, aye, I see them." ·

We advanced in procession, and the foppish personage realized that this was not according to plan. We would clash with the high spot of the Sylvies' performance.

He tried to halt us.

"Wait, you cramphs! Wait by the nine-towered serving tray of Beng Forlti."

Although adjured to stop by the patron saint of all waiters and waitresses, we marched on.

The guards, the musicians, the erotic performers, did not wear masks.

Everyone else did.

The glitter from the samphron-oil lamps' reflections blinded in silver.

Masks of Lem the Silver Leem—snarling silver leem masks!—adorned every face in that blasphemous assembly.

No need to describe the color or ornamentation of the robes of those feasting so merrily here!

High against the end wall the monstrous silver statue of the leem glittered down.

There was no iron cage, no little girl sacrifice in her white dress.

There were bloodstains upon the stone floor in a cleared area to the side.

Scuff marks in the stone flags told where the sacrificial block had been dragged away after the gruesome rites had been performed.

"Stop, you misbegotten cramphs, you spawn of Hodan Set! Stop or you will be flogged jikaider."

The foppish personage fairly danced with frustration, probably well knowing that if the servitors fouled up he would be flogged in that cruel crisscross fashion also.

Now I happened to be carrying a silver tray which bore a large, sugary, creamy confection, a ziggurat of a cake the Kregans call annimay cake. While undoubtedly too rich, too sugary, too creamy and altogether too fattening it is, even to a soured old forager like me, delicious.

About this time the bewildered and bothered chief steward, this overseer of the servers, woke up to the bizarre assortment of dishes we carried in so solemn a procession.

He fairly gobbled his alarm.

"What, what, what? You, there, with the bird . . . And you, a trifle. . . . And is that vosk and taylyne soup? What in the name of Llumino of the Sauces is going on?"

Pompino—he with the taylyne and vosk soup—said, "It is about time."

"Aye."

Murgon in his silver mask and his Brown and Silver robes sat at the head of the table, and the woman at his side must be Dafni—and she, too, wore the Brown and Silver and the silver leem mask covered her face. Murgon's two trusted thugs must be among that company, the Chulik, Chekumte the Fist, and the sly little apim, Dopitka the Deft, if they had not so far been slain. One or two of the silver masks angled in our direction and the lampglow glittered with inquiring menace.

"Let slip the hounds and let loose the shaft!"

Without more ado, having achieved complete surprise, we leaped into action.

The overseer of the servers had just reached the clear conclusion that all was not as it seemed with the servitors. He began to dance up and down in wrath.

"As certain as my name is Nath the Tureen, you will all be flogged—"

He went flying helter-skelter, this Nath the Tureen, as we threw the viands in all directions, tore out our weapons and leaped.

Pompino had marked Strom Murgon and for him he roared, shouting, his sword lifted. Cap'n Murkizon hurled the stuffed bird at the nearest table and followed it in a tremendous billow of outrageous clothes, smashed into the table, upending it. It crashed down on the feasters beyond.

Shrill screams sliced into the air and echoed from the ceiling. Viands crashed and splashed. The wicked silver glitter of swords rose to combat the evil glitter of silver leem masks.

The annimay cake sailed up into the air from my silver tray. It arched up and over. It descended.

Splat!

The two guards who rushed in from their position along the wall were smothered in the sugary gunk. Without masks to protect their faces the creamy cake blinded them.

Two swift chunks with the hilt disposed of them.

It seemed very necessary to me to make sure of the folk here who carried weapons. After that the more important task of sorting out the needlewoman might be attempted.

Well, we went at it with a will. Tinker-hammering uproar filled that opulent chamber.

No one felt inclined to pull their blows, to let these miserable specimens off the hook.

Men staggered away from the tables, their blood gushing over the brown robes. Men—and women, too—screamed and fought to win free, and Pompino and Cap'n Murkizon and Quendur roared into them. Nath Kemchug and Naghan the Pellendur and his guards smashed forward.

Some of the guards in their Lemmite uniforms fought well. Quendur had a right to do until Cap'n Murkizon reared up and his new axe went around in a flat and vicious arc, chunk into the side of Quendur's opponent.

Quendur didn't bother to shout a thankyou—he just swiveled and slashed the legs from the wight who attempted to brain Murkizon from the blind side.

Together, the two flailed their way on.

By this time, with a few of the guards coughing up their guts on the floor, I'd spotted the woman I took to be the doctor.

She wore the Brown and Silver and a silver leem mask covered her face. But she had not leaped up, either to escape or to fight. From the corner of my eye as I raced on I caught a fleeting glimpse of Murgon dragging Dafni along, and a couple of the guards making a valiant effort to protect their lord. Pompino was hard after them.

I fancied Pompino and the others had the situation well in hand now. Straight for the needlewoman I jumped.

She tilted her head to regard me and the mask caught the lamplight and gleamed dully.

"You would slay me, then?"

"Only if you deserve to be slain."

I backhanded a fellow off who tried to stick a short sword into my side, and he yowled and fell away, his sword arm shredded.

"You are a needlewoman?"

"That is why I sit here and do not take up a sword to strike you Unbelievers down."

I regarded her in that tumult of action and blood and death.

The fight was just about over. I do not believe I could have abandoned my comrades in the midst of action had they not been so signally successful. The sheer scale of

our surprise had granted us the victory from the moment
we had unsheathed swords and leaped.

Pompino was leading the lady Dafni back.

Her silver mask dangled from its straps. Her face was
distraught. She sobbed in convulsive, ugly heavings, and
she twisted and struggled and Pompino, gentle with her,
guided her to a seat.

"Bring wine for the Lady Dafni!"

So she was being attended to.

I called across.

"Hai! What of that rast Murgon?"

"Like the flat rock-basement inhabitant that he is, he
escaped through a secret door in the masonry."

"It closed up and snatched my sword away," yelled
Mantig the Screw, and he went busily off to find a fresh
weapon.

"So your great chief," I said to the needlewoman,
"abandons you. That is his honor."

"If I repeat a proverb, you will understand."

She had spirit, this lady doctor.

"Oh, aye. He'll run to fight another day. And when he
does, he may be killed, or he may run again. But you are
here and—"

"And in your power!"

I looked down. She could see my golden zhantil mask.
She could not see my expression, as I said: "Yes."

Her head jerked back.

"What do you want of me?"

"There is a man sore wounded. I need your skills and
your arts to attend him."

The leem mask swiveled sideways. She regarded that
luxurious banqueting hall where the blood stank rich
and smoking upon the yellow napery, upon the floor, upon
the bright tapestries. Bodies lay in grotesque positions.

"There are many who need my ministrations."

"Probably. But this man, you will attend first."

I held out my hand to assist her to rise, and she
disdained that brown and clutching claw and stood up.
With a flick she adjusted the brown robe.

I pointed to her silver-banded balass box.

"I will carry that for you, sana."

She laughed.

That startled me.

She laughed at my use of the honorific of sana, which

gave her the honor due to a sage, a mistress, in the arts of healing.

But, natheless, I picked up the box which would contain her unguents and her acupuncture needles and the medicines in which she would be skilled. I guided her sedately over a few corpses and around the spilled blood and so brought her into the kitchens where Rondas the Bold lay.

"Your name, sana?"

"I am called Shula the Balm."

"Well, Mistress Shula, here is your patient."

"He is a Rapa!"

I bent my head to glare at her, the zhantil mask glittering.

"He is a Rapa. I would suggest you remove that vile silver leem mask before you attend him. He is likely to thrust a dagger through your guts if he sees that obscenity above him."

Her hands, very white, very nervous, fluttered; then she began to unclasp the fastenings of the mask.

Well, even on Kregen you sometimes expect the ordinary, which is a foolish fault.

The capacious brown robes with their silver embroidery concealed and disguised her bodily form. I'd expected an apim woman.

I was wrong.

She was hiosmim. Oh, yes, her face bore resemblances to an apim face; but the pixie look, the width of the high cheekbones, the curve of the chin, the spacing of the eyes, all spoke eloquently of hiosmim blood. Her skin was white with a creaminess to the coloring vastly different from any chalk-white semblance. Her hair of a pale blue was confined in a silver band. About her clung an aura of calm, of competence, of that certain sureness of inner certainty that normally arouses complete trust.

In these moments her racial characteristics aroused in me only horror.

That such a woman, devoted, sure, blessed, should have been swayed by the cult of Lem!

But I would not allow doubt to enter my mind.

Or, if I did, it was to be refuted instantly by what I knew of the habits of the Lemmites.

Wordlessly, I pointed at Rondas.

At once, she opened her medical box and set to work.

CHAPTER THIRTEEN

Shula the Balm

"So much for his share of my agio!"

Jespar the Scundle crawled out from under a table and stood up. He chewed on a chicken bone. He was not the least whit abashed that he had not charged in with us and struck a blow. I, for one, could hardly fault him for that.

Shula the Balm looked up. Difficult, of course, to translate the facial expressions of one race into a meaning to another—did that wrinkling of the brow indicate anger, fear, contempt, amusement?

She said, "Tump. Hold this."

Jespar jumped.

He had been a free tump, a mining man, and then he had been slave. His instincts had been sufficiently overlaid by discipline to make him instantly reach forward and do as he was bid.

The woman barely acknowledged him.

The "this" he was requested to hold was the hideously blood-smeared dart embedded in Rondas the Bold. Acupuncture needles festooned our comrade and, thankfully, all his pain was eased away. He closed his eyes as the needlewoman began with her sliver of knife on his wound.

As she worked with an exactitude I found pleasing, she spoke: "If I save this man I assume I have your promise of my life?"

I pondered this—oh, the answer leaped fully formed into my head at once, of course—but I had no wish to allow any thoughts of mercy to devalue her due recognition of her position. This was not the shameful attitude it might be thought to be in a company of knights errant—any persons who followed Lem the Silver Leem put themselves beyond the pale of civilization at a stroke. . . .

Then: "Your life is of no consequence beside that of this man and of my comrades." I could hear myself mouthing the words—and I refused to regard them as despicable—and I went on in that grating tone: "But I am not in the habit of wantonly slaying little girls in white dresses or of offering up their hearts, still beating, to a filthy silver statue. You may perhaps live if you serve well."

Her fingers did not quiver. But her head bowed a trifle lower under the onslaught of my words.

She said, "It is time. Help the tump."

So with the keen knife easing the way, Jespar and I drew the cruel barb from Rondas.

His feathers were blood-spattered. The wound gaped.

"Hand me the box."

Jespar jumped to obey.

She took out unguents, bandages, began to dress the wound with a skill I admired.

"The bleeding will stop very soon. I have removed all the detritus. But the dressings must be changed frequently—"

"You will be alive, Shula the Balm, to see to that."

"I would suggest that you and your comrades bathe as soon as possible." Suddenly she turned that pixielike face up, and the tiny nose wrinkled. "You stink."

"Aye."

Footsteps on the flags of the kitchen heralded Pompino. As usual he was brilliant and heady, brushing up his whiskers, a fine foxy Khibil, master of the situation.

"They never knew what hit 'em!"

"Quite. I think Murgon merely evades his fate. The Lady Dafni?"

"A strange one, that. Oh, and she has stopped her eternal chatter for a space. She was confused. She resisted her rescue because of the golden zhantil masks."

"I see."

Pompino dangled his mask. The gold caught the lamplight, glimmering in that chamber of culinary splendor.

"The fanshos are tired, yet we can march back to the airboat. Can Rondas travel?"

I turned to the needlewoman.

"It would be better not to move him—" she said.

"Better, perhaps. But can we carry him safely?"

She hesitated.

I said: "I have conditionally promised this person her life, even though she is a Lemmite. She—"

"No lover of Lem should be allowed to live and breathe the same air as honest folk!"

Again was that a shadow across her face, a minuscule flinching back? I could not fathom this doctor—yet.

"Nevertheless, she will go with us to attend Rondas. Now, Pompino—are there more wounded?"

He grunted.

"Poor Faplon the Chuckle took a spear through the guts, and as he fell a sword half-removed his head. And Nath Kemchug lost half his pigtail—"

"I hate to think of what befell the wight who did that monstrous deed!"

"Bits of him lie here and there."

"As for Faplon the Chuckle—a pity. He was always cheerful, and a good Fristle."

"Yes. Otherwise, apart from a few scratches, we were too fast for them, thanks be to Horato the Potent."

True to their calling, our mercenary comrades now busily occupied themselves in collecting up all the plunder displayed on the tables and spilled onto the floor.

In a tremendous smother of white Quendur emptied out a flour sack. He darted back into the main hall and there he would quickly stuff the flour sack with golden cups and dishes, silver knives, ornate candlesticks. Strom Murgon did not stint himself when it came to the good things of life—in this instance the lavish furnishing for his table.

"Those two hirelings of Murgon's were not among the dead," said Pompino. "I turned the bodies over with them particularly in mind. Chekumte the Fist and Dopitka the Deft could not have been here. I'm certain sure no one else escaped with Murgon, apart from a hairy Brokelsh with one arm hanging off."

"Oh?"

"Aye. He carried a leather sack. Murgon almost ran him down escaping through that devilish slit in the wall."

Jespar the Scundle had, like me, received a liberal blessing of Rondas's blood when the dart pulled free. Now, as we went across to the sinks to wash, he looked nervous.

"My second cousin's wife's brother—Tangle the Ears. Masters—did you see a disgusting tump lying in his own blood among the corpses out there?"

Pompino laughed.

"No, Jespar."

"Hmf," sniffed Jespar. "It would be like him to be found dead drunk in the wine cellar."

Our two girl varterists had found a splendid tapestry which they were arguing over.

Wilma the Shot said: "It should be cut lengthwise."

"Not so, sister," said Alwim the Eye. "Cut it across."

"If you cut it across you will part the pictured peoples' heads from their bodies."

"But if you cut it down you leave almost all the gold thread in one half—"

"Maybe so. But it is more artistic—"

"Then who is to have the golden-heavy half?"

"Why," said Wilma, cheerfully: "You may have the golden section, sister. The picture is the important thing."

So, their argument settled in sisterly fashion, they chopped the priceless tapestry down the middle.

I wiped myself on a fluffy yellow towel and looked about.

"Time we were moving on, Pompino. I begin to fret over the airboat up aloft—"

"Agreed. We may have to thwack our rascals to make them move."

"They'll move."

A very few words proved sufficient to convince our comrades that it was time to go. A party carefully carried Rondas on an improvised stretcher. After a last look around that chamber of death, we started our march back to the voller.

Shula the Balm walked with a lissom swing beside Rondas's stretcher. She had applied unguents to bruises and stuck a few needles in furry hides, here and there, to ease the pain of wounds. But, mercifully so, we had suffered miraculously few injuries.

Jespar's relative, Tangle the Ears, had not been discovered, drunk or sober. The little tump knew a straight way from the banqueting hall to the yard above. He mumbled something about generations of tumps coming here to pay their taxes to the Marsilus family, damned iniquitous taxes, he said, and we strode on feeling more and more confident.

Although we kept a sharp lookout we saw no sign of Strom Murgon.

Nothing Pompino or the crew had been able to do had opened the secret panel in the wall. No doubt dusty passageways led through the fabric of the building to a hidden doorway. By this time Murgon should be well away.

No one minded that too much.

That villain would run upon his fate soon enough.

For the time being he must be considered out of the game. We had rescued the Lady Dafni—again!—and before long she would be reunited with Pando.

So up we went and entered the last corridor that would take us to the yard upon the roof.

The various unpleasant traps Jespar pointed out we were thankful to avoid. We would have had a much harder journey of it this way, even, than we had going the tortuous route we had followed.

Two guards, Brokelsh both, lay on the stone, their hairy bodies slack in death.

At the far end of the corridor the opening glowed with a penumbra of light. Outside, the twin suns of Scorpio were rising, casting down their mingled streaming light upon the world of Kregen.

From the shadows a voice, hard and yet gasping, said: "Hold! Stand fast, or you are dead men!"

We had seen the shafts transfixing the bodies of the Brokelsh guards.

"Hai!" called Pompino. "It's us! Hold fast your shaft, Larghos."

"Quidang! You are well met—"

We hurried forward, alarmed by the hoarseness of Larghos's voice.

He stood in the shadows of a groined arch, his bow lifted. As we approached he lowered the weapon.

"It's this stupid wound I took, when we snatched the treasure upon the quay. It bothers me."

Brisk, efficient, Pompino said: "We have a needlewoman with us, Larghos. A Mistress Shula. She will treat your old wound, even if she is a misbegotten Lemmite."

Larghos did not look well. His face held a grayish cast I, for one, did not like.

"I welcome that, horter Pompino. There have been only those two Brokelsh who came by. No one else. I own I am glad to see you." He peered at the stretcher. "Rondas?"

"A bad stroke; he will survive. Let us all go along to the airboat."

Cap'n Murkizon took a firm grasp on Larghos, supporting him, and as we covered the last few paces out to the suns shine, started to tell him of our adventures.

Out in the yard, with the early light, palest lemon and shimmering apple-green, suffusing the stones with a luminescence, we stopped.

We looked about, gaping.

There was no voller there waiting for us.

Pompino quelled the outcry.

He gestured widely, fingers stabbing upwards.

"What a pack of famblys!" He laughed, expansively. "The lady Ros heard Larghos the Flatch dealing with those two stupid Brokelsh. She has taken the airboat up to be on the safe side—"

Larghos pushed himself straight from the embracing grip of Murkizon's arm.

"No, horter Pompino. No." He wet his lips. "After I dispatched them I went back to the flying boat. It was still here, and the lady Ros was talking to the lady Nalfi—"

A buzzing arose then, of unease. Quendur stepped up.

"And Lisa the Empoin?"

Larghos shook his head.

"I did not see her. The lady Ros said she had ventured down a passageway again—"

"Again!"

"Aye. She was most wroth that you had forbidden her to accompany you. The lady Ros and she went down this passage and came back. Then the lady Lisa the Empoin went again. The lady Ros went after her as I came back to my post."

"This I do not like," quoth Pompino. He brushed at his whiskers; but the gesture was far removed from his usual confident flourish.

I looked up and about the morning sky. A few clouds offered some cover; I did not think they would have concealed a voller for the time I searched the sky.

No sign of the airboat—and no sign of Dayra.

In a hard and exceedingly unpleasant voice, Quendur the Ripper said: "Which way, good Larghos, did the lady Empoin take? Which particular passage?"

Larghos gestured.

"That one."

Without another word, Quendur started off for the indicated passage leading from the yard at right angles to the one we had adventured down. Instantly, I was at Quendur's side. Together, we plunged into the dimness.

A few slotted windows at the side were mostly blotted by choking festoons of spiders' webs. A little light seeped through, mottling the dusty floor with ruby and vermilion.

Quendur's sword snouted forward. His fist looked hard and knobbly, and the patterned light painted a trick upon his face, so that he looked like a puppeteer's dangled nightmare. I paced him.

Shouts reached us as we moved along, distant at first and as Quendur—recognizing those calls for help—broke into a frantic sprint, growing louder every second. We found Lisa the Empoin neatly entrapped. Cobwebbed spider strands engulfed her, strands cunningly interwoven with thongs and slender iron-linked chains. The whole lot had fallen upon her from the ceiling as she brushed through.

She saw Quendur and the color rose in her face.

Quendur put his hands on his hips and his sword angled up alarmingly.

"So, my lady, this is how you amuse yourself when I am away—"

"Stop jabbering, you great buffoon, and get me out! Oh, and there are spiders about as big as soup plates you would do well to avoid—or squash instantly." She glanced to the side.

She'd squashed one of the creepy horrors, fairly pulping him. A thin yellowish ichor trailed from the broken body. The thing *was* as big as a soup plate.

As Quendur, tight-lipped, started to cut Lisa free, I peered around, sword and feet ready to pierce or squash.

"The chains—" she said. And then: "My love—I am—"

"Save your breath, Lisa the Empoin."

"But, my heart—"

"You—" Quendur let rip a long groaning sigh. "You are the most obstinate of women!"

"Yes."

"And you are right. I cannot break the chains."

"There are no skeletons that I can see lying about," I pointed out, helpfully. "So they did not expect to leave a victim entrapped here. Perhaps those two Brokelsh were patroling this way—"

"Probably."

"The chains—"

"I am going back to the yard," I said. Before they had time to register their surprise or disapproval, I went on briskly: "If Cap'n Murkizon will lend us his axe—"

"Hurry, Jak Leemsjid," Quendur said.

I hurried. Murkizon came back personally and hacked Lisa free of the chains. As she staggered forward into Quendur's arms, the gallant Captain Murkizon said: "The notches in my blade are well bought for the sake of so fine a lady, aye, by the scabrous belly and verminious hair of the Divine Lady of Belschutz!"

"I will buy or obtain the finest axe for you, Cap'n Murkizon," said Quendur. "And with it goes my thanks."

He did not look at me.

I knew the unspoken thoughts seething away in Quendur's mind, as they must soon seethe away in all my comrades' skulls when they heard this tale.

Lisa cut that knot—thankfully.

"The lady Ros tried to make me return with her—and I would not. Quendur—I own sometimes I am headstrong and foolish—but—"

"You are," quoth Quendur the Ripper, firmly.

We walked back along the passageway and Murkizon trod flat-footed upon a scuttling spider, and thought nothing of it. I swallowed and said: "Lisa—the lady Ros?"

"When I would not go back to the yard with her she said that the Lady Nalfi was probably more at risk than I was.

"She was perturbed, and I shall apologize to her, for I put her in a difficult position."

"If she has returned in the flier."

That meant Quendur had to explain our predicament to Lisa.

"Ros Delphor would never desert us." Lisa spoke as firmly as Quendur. "I have talked with her, as she with me. She is a lady—oh, I know how we all laugh. But it is sooth. There must be another explanation for her absence. . . ."

She stopped herself speaking then.

By Krun! Didn't I know there could be another explanation! A dark, horrible and altogether unbearable explanation. . . .

CHAPTER FOURTEEN

"Prepare for the Scorpion!"

Pompino, twirling his whiskers, said, "I have not burned a temple for some time and I am beginning to feel chilly."

Pando, bright, arrogant, hugely relieved, said: "I thank you again for the safety of the lady Dafni. I am at your disposal when it comes to burning the Lemmites' temples."

We'd marched down from Korfseyrie and met up with Pando's force, flushed from their forced march. We had slept off the effects of our adventure, we had eaten enormously, and Pompino was fretting to be up and about and doing.

Of course, I shared his views. But my concern of a father for Dayra fretted away at me.

Pompino scoffed at my fears.

"Ros Delphor can look after herself, Jak! Perhaps the airboat—wonderful though it truly be—developed some defect and drifted off with the wind."

"The lady Ros," said Pando, "is a formidable lady, in all Pandrite's truth."

"So—" I began.

They wouldn't hear of querulous hearts.

Larghos the Flatch was so down in the mouth we all guessed that his concern for the lady Nalfi weighed on him far more than the aftereffects of his wound. Shula the Balm treated him, so he would recover; he shared with me the agonies of not knowing what was befalling a loved one.

The camp we'd made in the woods served us well enough for the time we recouped our strength. Now Pompino, mindful of the long journey entailed in reaching the nearest likely site of a temple, itched to be off.

Rondas the Bold made a terrible scene when we told

him he'd have to go along with Kov Pando's party back to Plaxing.

"I do not skulk when there is work to be done, by Rhapaporgolam the Reiver of Souls!"

He appealed with Rapa fervor to Shula the Balm, his feathers whiffling, his beak snouting, his crest wild.

"If they tie you upon a beast so you do not fall off, you might go, Rapa. I would not answer for your life."

"I do not ask you to, Lemmite! That commodity, precious though it is, is now back in my keeping."

"So be it."

Rondas the Bold, therefore, would come with us.

Nath Kemchug, a dour, hard, merciless Chulik, said, "If you fall off, Rondas, I will catch you." Then, with a thumb along a tusk, glistening it up, he added, "And I'll tie you back on so tight your eyeballs will pop."

We were all glad that Rondas had recovered so speedily. He expressed his gratitude to us. In our turn we chaffed at him—for Rapas do, indeed, possess their own weird brand of humor—and the moment that might have become mawkish passed in amiable insult.

The crafy Ift, Twayne Gullik, spent only the briefest of times at the camp, and then he went back at once to Plaxing with his people, claiming that his duties called him.

Jespar stared after the cavalcade.

"And good riddance," he said, unknowing that he was overheard.

Pompino and I, who had gone a little way off, ignored that. Tump and Ift—well, the up and the down, the dark and the light—and perhaps the twain never would meet.

Pompino started, suddenly, and he looked up with such an involuntary look of apprehension, my sword was halfway out of its scabbard before I, too, saw what had startled him.

Up there, floating in tight hunting circles, the giant golden and scarlet raptor of the Star Lords looked down upon us.

That bird was undeniably beautiful. Its golden feathers gleamed with a brilliance outshining mortal gold. The scarlet of its coat of feathers emphasized that glitter of gold around its throat and eyes. The wicked black talons outstretched, scarlet tipped, golden tipped, raked down as though to seize us up and rend us to pieces.

The Gdoinye up there circled, his head tilted, survey-
ing us. He was the messenger and spy of the Star Lords.
They watched us, those superhuman near-immortal men
and women, they watched us.

Pompino, I often fancied, must have fallen to his knees
when first the Gdoinye appeared to him, and spoke, and
gave him orders. Now he remained standing; but he
remained stiff, quiveringly alert, receptive, a perfect tool
in the hands of unknowable despots.

My own relations with the Gdoinye had been of an
entirely different character—altogether on a coarser plane.
My reactions and antics alarmed my Kregoinye comrade.

Both of us were well aware that no one else in our
company could see or hear the messenger from the
Everoinye.

The bird swung lower, cutting across the face of Zim,
the giant red sun, and so turned himself into a wedge of
blackness against the light. He volplaned out, turned,
glinting in radiance, arrowed down for us.

"Scauro Pompino, known as the Iarvin!"

The Gdoinye's hoarse croak reached us with clarity as
he circled, hovering.

"Dray Prescot, Onker of onkers!"

"Aye, you rascally, injurious, supercilious bird of ill
omen!" I roared back. And, in the old way, I shook my
fist up at him.

He croaked a squawk that might have been a laugh.

"Jak! Jak!" Pompono fairly bristled with anxiety.

"We are on our own time now," I said. "We choose to
oppose Lem the Silver Leem because it appears a seemly
thing to do. We know the Everoinye also oppose the
Lemmites; but we were not sent here by the Star Lords—"

"Cease your stupid babble, Onker!"

I glared up at the bird. Pompino put a hand to his
whiskers; but for some reason failed to brush them up in
the old arrogant way.

"Jak!" He almost writhed in his alarm and embarrass-
ment. Then he tilted his foxy head back and called up:
"We obey your commands. We burn the temples of
Lem—what—?"

"Yes, Pompino the Iarvin, there is yet more!"

"Certainly!" I bellowed up. "Certainly, there is always
more! And what help do we ever receive from you?"

"Jak!"

"You do not understand the help you are given. You are human. I am not here to bandy words. I am here to warn you of a summons. Prepare yourselves."

"Damned considerate of you!"

Well, it was, really, given the Star Lords' usual endearing habit of plunking me down naked and unarmed in a devilish tricky spot to pick their hot chestnuts out of the fire.

The Gdoinye winged up, a blurring of gold and scarlet.

"Prepare for the Scorpion!"

His blunt head pointed up, those powerful wings shredded the air, in a smother of wingbeats he lifted away, dwindled to a dot against the brightness of the sky, vanished.

"Humph!" I said. I did not spit.

"Jak—you run hard upon a leem's nest!"

"Oh, the Gdoinye and I have sharpened many a rapier together. I admit that talking to him is like saddling a zhantil—but, all the same, he has warned us."

"I believe this will make our task, as it were, official in the eyes of the Everoinye. Thanks be to Pandrite the All-Glorious."

"It was official enough for me before, by Chusto!"

The others in the camp were going about their duties without taking the slightest notice of us. The Star Lords were perfectly capable of putting the whole of Kregen under a spell if they wanted to, I did not doubt. That they did not do so, that they worked toward the fulfillment of their plans through fallible human tools like us, was all a part of their mystery. I did not think—then—that I would ever penetrate that mystery. I persuaded myself that it did not concern me. I refused to worry over it. By Vox! I had enough worries of my own, what with Dayra going off and Opaz-alone knowing where she was. All the same, there had in these latter days been a growing rapport between the Star Lords and myself I had viewed with interest—with unease, of course, and with confidence for the future.

Now, it seemed, we had a fresh task set to our hands.

"Jak—" began Pompino.

I turned to look at my comrade. I turned slowly.

I'd taken the name of Jak for perfectly obvious reasons—reasons I have explained and that are easily understood. But, sometimes, it irked me, this answering to another

name. My name is plain Dray Prescot. I may be the Lord
of Strombor and a Krozair of Zy, which privileges and
responsibilities I take seriously. I was also Emperor of
Vallia, King of Djanduin, Strom of Valka, a whole pretty
kite-tail of titles and folderols. But, all the same. . . .

"Yes?"

"Once again the Gdoinye did not call you Jak. He
would know that you are now Jak Leemsjid."

"Of course he'd know, the cunning, onkerish—"

"Jak!"

Instinctively, Pompino glanced up. No doubt he expected lightning to blast down for my impiety. Pompino
dealt with the Star Lords on the basis that they were
supernal gods, demanding and worthy of obedience. He
was privileged to serve them. And they'd rewarded him.
Their machinations had brought the gold into his fists,
gold with which he'd bought his fancy fleet of ships.

As far as I knew, they'd not put a single copper ob my
way.

"Jak—why does the Gdoinye call you by the name of
the Emperor of Vallia, a name which you adopted as a
ruse long ago, when he knows the truth?"

I did not pluck my lower lip; I did not scratch my head.
I did not narrow my eyes on my comrade. Had I done all
those things they would have been perfectly proper.

"Well, Pompino . . ." I began. Then, as Seg Segutorio
would have said in his fine free way, I also said: ". . . My
old dom. It's like this."

And then I stopped.

No. No, I wouldn't shatter our relationship. As I had
surmised earlier, if I told Pompino the truth, he'd never
regard me in the same comradely way again. How could
he? If I was an emperor, then he'd have to start treating
me like an emperor, like one of the lordly beings of
Kregen, and I detested that. I valued Pompino. Perhaps,
when the situation was clearer, he might know, and then
we would work out a modus vivendi. For now—no. No, I
couldn't tell him the truth.

"Well, Jak Leemsjid?"

Now we had talked together of our experiences before-
time with the Star Lords. I'd been circumspect with
Pompino, anticipating he had not penetrated to the Star
Lords' hugely vaulted chamber of scarlet, seen the world
spread out below, ridden in one of their hissing chairs,

understood just a trifle of their plans. So he knew somewhat of my history regarding the Everoinye.

I said: "Must be because that was the first name they knew me by. They don't have the sense to get up to date."

"They know everything!"

"So they must forget a lot, mustn't they?"

"That, I cannot believe."

It sounded lame, even to me.

I tried again.

"The Everoinye were once human, as we are. I am sure they still possess a sense of humor. It may be vestigial. I think they amuse themselves by thus dubbing a poor wight like me with the name of the emperor of Vallia—"

"A most puissant and terrible man!"

"Oh, aye."

"He was dreadfully severe on the slavers in Vallia. His name is not one lightly to be conjured with. If ever you venture up into Vallia, Jak, you had best beware."

I said, and I blurted it out before my stupid babbling tongue could be halted: "One day, Pompino, I look forward to the time when you and I go in friendship to Vallia."

His bushy, foxy eyebrows rose.

"Oh?"

I blustered it out.

"Surely. There must be fine pickings there."

And I laughed, forcing myself, as a free-roving reiver and paktun would laugh at the thought of loot.

Pompino, severely, said, "If you try any tricks in Vallia these days, the emperor will put you down, cut off your head, dangle you over the walls of his stupendous deren in Vondium—Jak, Jak! Think on!"

"Well, there's a damned army forming in Port Marsilus, paid by gold from somewhere—gold that was once in our possession. When that army sails for Vallia, the story might be different."

"You would join that army against Vallia?"

"Join it?" I pretended to ponder. Then: "Aye, Pompino! I'd join it. Then I would sabotage it and destroy it and scatter it to the winds. Why, then, man, I'd go up to this high and mighty Dray Prescot, Emperor of Vallia, and stare him in the face, and demand a fitting recompense for saving his empire for him!"

And Pompino guffawed at the conceit.

He sobered. "If we are to be snatched up by the Scorpion of the Everoinye then I must warn Cap'n Murkizon and the others. They will have to make their way back to the ship."

"Aye."

Pompino nodded and walked off, moving briskly, going among the trees toward the camp.

I stood for a moment, all my thoughts of Dayra making me feel the miserable stupid fool I really was, that fool, that onker, that I was dubbed by the Gdoinye.

As I stood there the blue radiance grew about me.

The coldness of an arctic wind cut through every fiber of my body, the silence of a rushing wind drowned thought. The world fell away. I saw above me, towering and enormous, the gigantic blue outlines of the Scorpion, immense, awful, and then I toppled away into the blue radiance of the Star Lords' commands.

CHAPTER FIFTEEN

Gold Mask vs. Silver Masks

Sometimes the Star Lords procrastinated unbearably in their casual dumping of me down into action. Often and often I'd find myself in some desperate situation, quite without a clue, unable instantly to decide exactly what the Everoinye were demanding of me. They acted like this, I was more than half convinced, not out of malice but out of sheer indifference.

This time there was no misunderstanding.

Normally the Star Lords catapulted me into danger naked, unarmed, and half-bedazzled from the effects of the blue radiance, the baleful form of the gigantic Scorpion and the stomach-unsettling topsy-turvy fall through nothingness.

This time I felt limber, alert, ready for what might befall.

I needed to be.

By Zair, I needed to be!

I was, as usual, naked and unarmed.

Still the Everoinye must have sensed the lessening of regard for them that would have been engendered had they provided me with a spear, a helmet, a shield. They summoned, I went and did.

But—this time—there was something new.

In the rough canvas bag dangling on its cord over my shoulder snugged a hard, metallic object.

Without thinking twice—in all the uproar that surrounded me—I drew out the golden zhantil mask and snapped the straps about my head. I glared out through the eyeholes.

The scene was cut straight from nightmare.

The cavern lofted into purple shadows, bruised and swollen. Torchlights fluttered against that encompassing presence. The leering silver image of the Leem lowered over all, high against the far wall, silver glints striking and sparking from its body.

The iron cage stood empty. The door opened onto a stone ledge. On this ledge two acolytes of Lem the Silver Leem drew on the eager form of a little girl clad in a white dress.

Candy juice smeared her chin.

She was laughing.

Below, to the side, the altar crouched. Dark, misshapen, stained, it humped a blot of blackness against the torchlights.

The worshipers all wearing their silver masks swayed and gyrated, caught up in the expectations of the moment. The butcher-priests stood beside the altar. Their assistants held the implements of their trade upon cushions. The air stifled.

And the stink was diabolical.

I was one man, alone, naked and unarmed.

The worshipers mustered upward of a hundred. The priests and their assistants and acolytes another thirty or so.

Even as I started forward I was saying to myself but so that the damned Star Lords—wherever they were!—might hear: "Right, Star Lords. You've dropped me into a real beauty this time! By Vox! What a mess!"

A knee in the back of a fellow who was clutching at the woman next to him, ready for the bloodletting to follow, sent him toppling. Before he fell the thraxter in the scabbard at his waist was gripped in my fist.

I hit the next fellow a nasty slash along the neck and swiveled immediately to hack down his companion.

Run—run! Straight for the altar and the cage and the girl sacrifice! Run as I'd never run before—get into them, as Cap'n Murkizon would roar: "Hit 'em, knock 'em down, tromple all over 'em!"

The pandemonium began as I legged it, spreading from my hurtling body as the ripples spread from the thrusting prow of a swifter of the Eye of the World.

People tried to stop me.

They were cut down as the reaper cuts corn.

They saw the blazing gold of the zhantil mask.

Shocked cries burst out.

"The Golden Zhantil masks! Kill him! Kill!"

At least the Star Lords had had the sense to dump me down at the back of this unholy crew. They'd not seen me arrive, or don the mask. Now they saw a fleeting naked figure roaring along, cutting left and right, lopping heads, disemboweling, amputating limbs, the glinting glory of the zhantil mask ferocious upon them.

They crushed in to prevent my onward movement and to slay me.

Swords whipped up. Men and women screamed and gesticulated and tried to get at me.

I did not hang about.

The thraxter snapped off clean.

I hit a corpulent bastard over the head with the hilt and took his sword and degutted his crony at his side. The next two went down, the next reeled away with his face reflecting the effects of a foot in the guts, and I roared on.

It was all a blur, of course, a blur of action and movement, of the silver twinkle of swords and the quick spurt of dark red blood. Even then I don't believe I thought that I would never surface from this dank spot. There was no time for coherent thought. As each fresh opponent or pairs or threes or fours of opponents presented themselves they had to be taken on their merits. What the floor looked like in the wake of that intemperate bloody bashing onslaught I hesitate to contemplate.

I do recall that one thought hit me with scarlet intensity.

Where the hell was Pompino in all this frantic bedlam?

Had the Star Lords fouled up again?

Nobody of this ripe bunch possessed a bow, or, at least, no one shot at me.

One fellow hurled a stux and the javelin flew straight.

I took it out of the air with my left hand. I did not return it whence it came, a favorite trick of the Krozairs. Instead I lobbed it at the Chief Priest in his brown and silver robes and his ornate mask, the butcher knife in his hands. It sheared through his neck, half-severing it. I was disappointed his head did not fall off.

The Brown and Silver at his side jumped away, flinging up his hands in horror. But he didn't drop his own cunning little instrument of torture.

In the next half-dozen heartbeats I was past the chained-off area separating the main hall from the preserve of the priests. Here the incense stank away, stiflingly.

There was time—just—to throw two of the torches at the brown draperies, and then I leaped for the man who was now turned away from the fallen body of his chief. The other acolytes ran. I hit the second in command over the head—not too hard—hurdled him and scooped up the girl.

Two hard and unmerciful blows disposed of her guards.

The second-in-command staggered. I put the girl down—of course she was crying now—and said: "It is all right. Stand still."

I put an inch and a half of the thraxter into the second-in-command's guts and said: "Where is the way out?"

The repulsive idiot must have imagined I was setting up a bargain with him, making a compact.

"Behind the drapes there," he babbled. The sword must have been tickling him up. He wriggled like an insect on a pin. He pointed painfully. "There."

I finished him—and he still clutched the shiny instrument he would have used to put this girl child to so much pain—snatched up the sacrifice, and hared for the drapes.

Another stux hit the wall beyond as I wrenched the panel open.

We bundled through into dimness relieved by mineral-oil lamps at intervals. The air smelled stale and musty and yet clean by comparison with the stinks in that chamber of abominations. The door snapped shut. There seemed no way of bolting or barring it, so I just ran full tilt up the corridor.

The girl sacrifice, following the usual habits of girl sacrifices rescued against their wills, was yelling her head off and banging her heels against me.

The corridor opened into a square stone-cut chamber.

The congregation would be after me like a pack of leems.

The Chulik in the chamber, clad in leather armor with brown and silver flourishes, seeing me, immediately drew his sword and dropped into the on guard. He was ready for a pleasant foining match before he dispatched me.

The point of my flung thraxter took him in the throat. The blade punched on, ripping tendons and throat and all to smash in a welter of blood.

I ran on without stopping, scooped his sword up, went racing on along the far corridor.

Howls from back down the passage echoed from the

stone walls. The helter-skelter rush and hammer of feet roared after me. I fled on, carrying my cargo in her white dress as carefully as I could. Blood spattered the dress from the splashes and stains covering me. She was blubbering away now, a fist stuffed into her mouth and her nose all running and I felt for her, I felt for her. But that mob of hyenas baying after us—if hyenas bay—had to be outdistanced before we could stop. Outdistanced—for I was not sanguine of slaying them all, much though that would have cleansed the world of Kregen.

Steps hewn from the rock led up.

A few lanterns glowed to point out the broken treads and the darkly greasy patches where water seeped. The smell of the earth, dank and rich and sweet, began to oust the charnel-house stench of the chamber of worship and sacrifice with its unholy freight of incense and blood.

Through her sobs the child gasped out: "Put me down, put me down! Let me go!"

Now the treads were fashioned of wood, cutting through the dark earth, and my feet hit them with the hard smack of callused skin.

In these frantic moments of flight there was just no way of explaining, and my concern for the child had to be adjusted with what might appear to be the same callousness that affected my feet. She had been promised sweets and candies, a pretty white dress, and these goodies she had received. To be snatched from them by a naked hairy sweating devil in a glinting gold zhantil mask! No, oh, no, explanations at this moment could never explain.

The wooden door at the head of the stairs was not guarded from the inside, whereat my heart sank, for I judged it would be bolted and guarded from the outside.

The only way to find out was to put a shoulder to it and heave.

The door resisted.

I felt—I felt that demeaning rush of blood to the head, the scarlet curtain, the furious obsessive rage that trembles all along the muscles and bursts out in blinding ferocity.

I smashed at the door.

It flew open and the mingled emerald and ruby radiance of Kregen flooded in.

The splintered ends of the shattered bar thumped to

the ground. Clutching the girl sacrifice, my sword snouting, I leaped through the opening.

The two Chuliks who had been lounging on the wooden bench beside the door that let into the grassy bank scrambled to their feet. They wore the brown and silver and leather harness and they'd been playing at the Game of Moons. The pieces went flying. The Chuliks ripped out their swords and jumped for me silently.

Like all Chuliks I'd known, they were quick, professional fighting men. There was no chance of repeating my trick with a flung thraxter here. They were on me in a twinkling.

They did not attack one after the other like actors in a play who must never harm the hero; they leaped in together.

Tackling two Chuliks is difficult enough, Vox knows, without the encumbrance of a squealing, wriggling, kicking girl-child in your free arm. I dumped her down, yelled: "Stand still!" and ripped into the Yellow Tuskers.

They were good—well, that is a stupid remark! Any Chulik who goes overseas and takes employment as a paktun is good. No thought of fancy work entered my head. This had to be quick—damned quick, by Krun.

The grass afforded firm footing, so that we three could leap and pirouette and strike and withdraw with ease. They whipped in side by side and I avoided the first blows and curled my blade in and the left-handed one contemptuously foined me off. I had to skip and jump to miss his comrade's slash. The next onset went much the same way, although as in a mirror, for the right-hand one parried and the left-hand one struck. That round, like the first, ended with us fronting across the grass, warily seeking an opening, circling.

Of course, they tried to circle me from each side.

This was more like it.

They had to split up so that one could go clockwise and the other widdershins. They'd crush me between them as an ear of grain is crushed in the mill.

So they thought.

Without hesitation I rushed upon the left-hand fellow, making a bit of a pantomime of it, not actually screeching a war cry, but making enough of a menacing growling challenge to set the Chulik quivering.

As I thus rushed on him his companion, invisible at my back, let out a yell.

"Hold him, Changa!"

This fellow before me whirled up his thraxter, and a wild light came into his yellow face. His tusks were banded with silver. He set himself to meet my attack and, so I guessed, deal with me before his comrade arrived, and thus gain the kudos, what some Kregan warriors call the *absteilung*.

Without the shadow of a doubt, the other Chulik was haring across the grass toward my back, hungering for his share in what *absteilung* there was to be gained from one naked apim warrior.

I halted. I whirled.

The onrushing Chulik, all froth and foam, eyes glaring, tusks flecking spittle from his gaping mouth, gasping with the effort, reared up, sword high.

The one called Changa screeched.

"Beware, Tincho, beware. . . ."

I slid the blade into Tincho, twisted, withdrew, and instantly, without thought, flung sideways and snatched the thraxter aloft. Changa's blow clanged down. Then it was a twist, a thrust, another ugly twist, and a withdrawal.

Slowly, they collapsed. Each mirroring the other's actions, they fell to their knees. The swords dropped from lax fingers. Together, they pitched forward onto the grass, sprawled, limp and done for.

One—the one called Changa—managed to gasp out: "By Likshu the Treacherous . . . the apim fooled us . . ."

I looked down at them.

"By the Black Chunkrah," I said, and the sadness tinged my voice. "I salute you both, Chuliks."

The blood dripped from the thraxter.

It was the work of a moment to strip a length of brown cloth free and wind it about me. I looked about, and if I say my breathing was even and steady, do not be deceived.

The bank rose at my side with the smashed open door leading to the horrors within. Within a few moments horrors on two legs would come roaring out of that cavern seeking my blood.

Below me down the hill spread a tree-dotted expanse leading to the sea. The light of the suns sparkled on that sea. Just what sea it might be in all of Kregen I could not then know.

A seaport nestled in a bay with a spit of land to give protection. The roads were clustered with shipping. Away to the right on a flat grassy area of considerable extent the long ordered rows of tents of an army glistened in the light.

The scents of grass and trees came pleasantly to my nostrils. And a scampering white dot on twinkling bare legs skipped heedlessly down the grassy slope toward the town.

Picking up my sword, I followed.

CHAPTER SIXTEEN

A price for Carrie

"Twelve gold pieces, my friend, and I'll throw in an extra five dhems."

Carrying the girl sacrifice—her name she had whispered was Carrie—I tried to brush past in the crowded souk. The fellow with his black chin beard and gold chains and oily hair was persistent.

"Come now, my friend! I know why you are here! You cannot do better than deal with me, Honest Nath Ob-eye the Trancular. Fifteen gold pieces, then—"

He wore a patch over his left eye. His clothes were ornate if greasy, and he carried as well as a sword a whip coiled up over his left shoulder. If I sold Carrie to him he'd have no compunction in using that evil instrument on her. He'd do it in such a way as not to mark the merchandise. Slavers know how to strike in the pain ways.

Carrie and I had hidden in a brake of greenery as the pursuit from that devil's pit roared past. We'd cleaned ourselves up in a brook that led into the river that reached the sea where this seaport stood. Its name was Memguin and it boasted a powerful fortress. I'd never been here before. But I knew where we were.

By Krun! I knew!

The Everoinye had dumped me down in Menaham.

Menaham, whose inhabitants were known to their neighbors as the Bloody Menahem, stood immediately to the west of Pando's Bormark in Tomboram. Hereditary enemies, the two countries, and this bloody place had joined up willingly with Phu-Si-Yantong when, as the Hyr Notor, he had taken over in his crazy schemes to conquer the world.

Well, he was dead, the black devil.

But his evil legacy lived on.

"Look, dom," wheedled this Nath Ob-eye the Trancular. "There is no need to fear. I can see your situation at a glance. You are a poor man, and you have too many children. It is common, men and women being what they are and the good Pandrite blessing them with fecundity. Your girl will be placed in a good home where she will learn to sew and stitch and perhaps, if she has the aptitude, be trained in the arts. A harpist, a dancer, perhaps if she has the gifts of the gods an actress—the lords hereabouts are partial to—"

"Go," I said, "away."

"But, dom—"

The souk bustled with activity. The spicy scents rose, and with them the tantalizing odors of food reminded me that my insides were as hollow as a blown egg.

This unpleasant slaver tried a new tack as I pushed on through the throngs.

"Twenty gold pieces will set you up for life! Why—"

His offer was as nonsensical as to price as the situation was to my purposes.

I ignored him and settled Carrie more comfortably on my shoulder. She took considerable interest in the busy scene, with its sights and colors and scents and ceaseless activity, crying out in wonder from time to time. We'd got along in the time it had taken to reach Memguin. By Zair! And hadn't I had considerable experience lately in the psychological handling of bewildered little girl sacrifices?

"Look, my friend, let me put this to you. You have a sword. Perhaps you think of joining the army being raised by Kov Colun Mogper of Mursham?"

My intense interest was at once aroused. So that was the way of it! The treacherous Mogper was once more reaching a tentacle into my affairs. As to the sword, I had, perforce, to carry it naked in my free hand.

"Perhaps, my friend, you are not the girl's father at all. Perhaps you have stolen her away, kidnapped her for gain. If I call the watch. . . ."

A tall and emaciated thin Weul'til joined the proceedings from the side, using his furry mouth to fashion a grimace that passed for a smile. Not as tall as your average Ng'grogan, your average Weul'til; but skinnier, decidedly skinnier.

He adjusted his black clothes, shiny in their fashion, wriggled his antennae, and said: "Hai, Nath Ob-eye the Trancular! My friend—" Then to me: "I will match this thieving trader's best offer, aye, and increase it by five gold pieces—"

"You are too late, Lintin the Ancho! I was about to call the watch to apprehend this kidnapper."

I own I almost smiled.

This pair of villains waxing righteous about a kidnapping! For the Weul'til, at once serious, exclaimed: "A kidnap! Then let us call the watch at once."

No doubt they were working a variant of the badger game; but I had had enough. I restrained myself.

I looked at the pair of them, and if that old devilish Dray Prescot look flamed across my face and turned me into the semblance of a demon from the deepest pits of hell, I do not think I can be overly faulted.

"If you do not at once run away, you will not ever run again! Get going! *Grak!*"

Well, if I used that ugly word then, it fitted.

They flinched back, hovered—and then they grakked.

I'd not said "Bratch!" nor even the more correct "Schtump!" which means clear off or get out. No, I'd said grak, and this pair of villains had used that word enough times goading on their slaves to appreciate its meaning when applied to them by a wild, sword-armed fellow with a devil's face.

I walked on. The air smelled sweeter.

The little Och from whom I'd inquired directions had directed me through this souk—the Souk of Sweetmeats— as my quickest route. A few moments later I emerged from the arched roof onto the Street of Desires and so turned right onto the Boulevard of Pandrite All-Glorious.

This was a prestigious thoroughfare, and more than one passing person gave me a curious glance. Carriages passed with a flicker of wheels, people paraded in fine clothes, and among them the quick flitter of the slaves in their slave-gray breechclouts passed unnoticed. I carried a sword, and so was clearly not slave, for most if not all Kregans when trusting slaves with weapons dress them up in ornate and pompous finery so as to mark them. I pressed on until I reached the lime-washed wall with its wrought-iron gate, closed, set between stone pillars.

Each pillar was surmounted by a satyr carrying off a virgin, sculpted in bronze, most lifelike if twice life-size. I did not know whose embassy building this had been before the Times of Troubles. I pulled the bell ring.

Now—I was doing something I usually eschewed.

More often than not, of course, the Star Lords hurled me into action where what I was up to now was either not possible or against my best interests. I waited as the pleasant chiming of the bell dwindled to silence.

An almost naked wild-looking fellow, carrying a bare sword, with a girl child perched on his shoulder, might be an apparition not well-received at someone's front door.

That thought had scarcely crossed my mind, incensed by those two slavers in the souk and by concern for Carrie and that ill-starred army mustering under the command of one of the vilest rogues yet unhanged. I just rang the bell and waited for the porter. I'd convince him easily enough.

There was no need.

The door in the gatehouse opened smartly and a fellow with one arm trotted out across the gravel. He wore buff breeches and buff shirt with red and yellow banded sleeves. His face was red and purple, beetle-browed and cheerfully pugnacious. The empty red and yellow sleeve was pinned up defiantly across his chest like a sash.

"And what does a fellow like you want. . . ?" he began as he came up with Carrie and me.

He stopped.

He opened his mouth and closed it. His beetle-brows rose as though on stilts. He opened his mouth again and this time he got out: "Now may Opaz the Saver of Souls be praised!"

He fairly scuttled to the bar and lifted it with his one right hand with a smooth and powerful swing.

Then he slapped that right arm across his chest with rib-crushing force.

"Lahal, majister! Lahal and Lahal!"

CHAPTER SEVENTEEN

In the embassy

You cannot expect an emperor to know the name of every soldier in his army, an empress the name of every voswod in her aerial forces. Some of them are canny enough, like Napoleon, to have themselves briefed before a parade so that they can talk to a soldier and use his name in a familiar way. This builds the legend.

Well, by Vox, I knew a large, a very large number of people on Kregen, and once I'd met them I'd normally remember names and faces.

This one-armed ex-soldier, beaming away, his purple face an enormous smile, I did not know.

I would not prevaricate. So—I ruined one legend.

I said, "Lahal and Lahal. Your name?"

He looked not one whit disappointed, and, to be truthful, he'd have been a fool had he been.

"Llando the Ob-handed, majister, that was Llando the Pilinur, Bratchlin in the Sixth Kerchuri when we won the day at Kochwold!"

"Aye, Llando. When the Second Phalanx trembled, the Sixth Kerchuri saved the day. I do not deny it. The Third Phalanx. . . . You lost your arm there?"

"A hairy Clansman astride a vove would have chopped young Larghos the Fair, my sister's boy, had I not been quick . . ."

He wore three bobs on his chest, medals of campaign and valor. I nodded, gravely, saluting a brave man.*

He smiled easily. "I have my job here, gatekeeper, the pay is good, the company fine, and although we may be

---

* For the Battle of Kochwold see *A Life for Kregen*: Dray Prescot #19.—A.B.A.

in a nasty sort of land with uncommon nasty people in it, why, majister, one must do what one can, surely?"

"You are a philosopher, Llando. And you are right."

He beamed and swelled up as though to burst.

It did not occur to me then to ask why he was not more surprised at seeing me than he was at my appearance. Later I realized that the tales and stories of Dray Prescot, of how the emperor sallied forth in headlong reckless adventure clad in a red breechclout, wielding a deadly Krozair longsword, were part of the tapestry of life in Vallia.

That Dray Prescot, Emperor of Vallia, might turn up anywhere to join a fight, to rescue honest folk, to put down slavers, was an article of faith to Vallians. But they'd expect him to come leaping in with the scarlet breechclout flaming and that deadly silver brand a glitter of destruction before him. And here I was, in a miserable scrap of brown cloth and with a wide-eyed little girl perched on my shoulder!

Well, Llando the Ob-handed made no more of that, and soon I was escorted through into the embassy.

The ambassador, Strom Ortygna Felheim-Foivan, met me with immense kindness. He did not fuss; but he saw that the right things were done. A short, stout, abrupt man, he held two small estates down by the Great River in Vomansoir and was therefore one of Lord Farris's men. Farris and I were good comrades, and Felheim-Foivan an old acquaintance.

"The Little Sisters of Benediction have a chapel here, majister, they will care for this girl child admirably."

"Excellent, Ortyg."

We sat in his private withdrawing room, the remains of the repast still on the table, the silver dish of palines to hand, the wine standing ready. The suns declined and Carrie had been half asleep when the sisters carried her off.

"I admit, majister, to grave doubts when I was offered this post. Vallia and all of Pandahem have been hereditary enemies since times immemorial. But you have changed all that. The Bloody Menahem are an unpleasant lot; but I am growing to understand them better, and with understanding comes—"

"Liking?"

He chewed a paline, thinking. "Hardly that. But

tolerance. I know I speak perhaps out of turn. But the habits of a lifetime, to turn a phrase, are not easily changed."

"That is true."

We talked for a time on the problems of Vallia, how the island empire must fulfill its obligations to all the peoples not only of its own fair lands but also of the new allies we had made overseas. There were many men now in Vallia like this Strom Ortyg who had come to the fore in recent days when a great deal of the old corruption had thankfully been banished. He served Vallia to the best of his ability, and within the framework of his labors and understanding shared the visions of the future dominating the best minds. He had outfitted me in proper evening style, a comfortable robe of dark material, and also I took the opportunity of writing some of the letters that were once more overdue.

My anxiety—and that was too mild a word—over Dayra had to be put into perspective.

She was a big girl now.

The imperatives, as I saw them, were to regain contact with Pompino and our comrades, to continue the struggle against the Lemmites, to sort out Pando's problems with Strom Murgon, and to scupper the damned army they recruited against Vallia.

"Against Vallia, majister?"

Strom Ortyg paused with a paline halfway to his mouth. He stared at me. Then, heavily, he said: "This Kov Colun Mogper of Mursham is—is not a pleasant person. But I am assured he raises this army to march against Tomboram, their hereditary foes."

Picking up the point that interested me more out of curiosity, I asked Ortyg: "You have met this Mogper?"

"Aye—well, briefly, only. He is an elusive personage."

"Most."

The word came out dry and harsh.

As I waited, Strom Ortyg realized what was required and went on: "He is a brilliant man; merciless, resolute, dominated by a sense of his own importance and the bending to his will of all with whom he comes in contact."

"Yes. And?"

"His appearance, majister? Tall, strong, with features regular yet marked by his character. Fair of hair, I believe, and yet most unfair in all other things. He affects armor gilded so that he presents the semblance of a golden statue, an idol to be worshiped."

That was as good a description as I could expect of the man I had once seen riding amid his armed cronies.

I said: "If ever a lady called Jilian Sweet Tooth should seek your aid, Strom Ortyg, in the matter of this Kov Colun Mogper, you would earn my gratitude if you would afford her every assistance of which you are capable."

He looked at me a trifle oddly. Then he nodded.

"If ever the lady seeks my assistance, I will do all in my power to aid her. And with pleasure."

"Good. And now—" A knock at the door heralded a young lad, Tyr Stofin Vingham, with news that a Courier airboat had just arrived from Vallia. Moments afterward the Courier himself, Hikdar Naghan Veerling, walked in smartly. Clad in flying leathers, wearing the neat pin on his tunic fashioned into the likeness of a silver zorca that was the badge of the Vallian Courier Service, he bore a thick wallet of messages. Not quite in the same class as the merkers, these couriers; but close. He saluted, saw me, smiled, and said: "Lahal, majister, lahal, Strom Ortyg."

So, the next three hours or so were spent in dealing with the information brought by Naghan Veerling.

Vallia prospered, I kept up with the news, and I could send back my own letters and messages by a rapid route.

Of course, I did not fail to recognize this odd phenomenon I had encountered plenty of times before this. My people of Vallia did not seem the slightest bit surprised to see their emperor popping up in the most unlikely places. Wherever they went, well, if the emperor happened to be there too, wasn't that perfectly natural?

After all, by this time they knew that Jak the Drang, Dray Prescot, was not like your ordinary emperor.

So it was that, knowing young Hikdar Naghan Veerling was one of your high-powered tearaways, I said to him as we took a breather: "Naghan. Before you fly back to Vallia, are you game for a little excitement?"

"Of course, majister."

I grumped inwardly at that, this calm acceptance of whatever deviltry I might have in store for him. Still, that was your Vallian, oh so respectable to all when it pleased, and your right villain when pushed.

"Strom Ortyg," I went on, "if I might borrow a few of

your lusty lads of the guard detail. And anyone else in the embassy who would like to join. . . ?"

"Naturally, majister."

I stood up and looked down on them, at the desks with the papers and pens and inks, at the packets ready to be sealed. "Well. And aren't you interested in what you'll be doing?"

"We'll be off on an adventure with you, majister."

By Zair!

Naghan the Courier added: "Anyone fortunate enough to go on an adventure with Dray Prescot, Emperor of Vallia, is more than fortunate."

"Aye. He might get his fool self killed."

Naghan laughed.

"When I flew the old vollers, that was an occupational hazard."

As a Courier, a fellow spending his time flying airboats, he called them by their Havilfarese name, as was proper.

He rubbed his chin. "Nowadays, with these fine new vollers you have secured for us, majister, life is more than a little tame."

"Give me a few burs sleep. Then gather the lads together, armed and ready, and we'll set off."

"Quidang!"

I looked at them.

"And still you do not ask where?"

"When the time is right you will tell us."

"I'll tell you now. We're off to burn a stinking temple to Lem the Silver Leem. That's where!"

So it was that, before the last of the seven Moons of Kregen was paled into a luminous echo in the sky by the glory of the twin suns, Zim and Genodras, we went up to that place of evil in the hill, entered through the door that had been hastily repaired, leaving four Chuliks set to guard the stable when the horse had bolted, stretched upon the grass, and so burned the vile place.

We found no worshipers, no interior guards, no acolytes or priests. We found no unnatural women preparing children for torture and sacrifice. We found no little girl children penned and waiting.

What we did find we burned.

Then, as the Suns of Scorpio flooded down in shimmering veils of color, we marched down the hill and so by devious ways regained the Vallian Embassy.

No one saw us.

Which was as well for them.

The men who had done the work had previously been informed by me of the nature of the beast they burned.

As a consequence they decided to celebrate, to hold a small thanksgiving service dedicated to Opaz the Just, and then in continuation that evening to hold a right roaring shindig. At this they drank and sang and told stories and the ladies present danced turn and turn and joined in the celebrations and, in short, everyone had a rousing good time. Which is the Kregan way.

There was no doubt in my mind that Strom Ortyg Olavhan of Felheim-Foivan ran an efficient, brisk and as far as the circumstances of being stationed in an unfriendly country allowed, a happy embassy.

Despite having only one arm, Llando the Ob-handed still had two legs and a voice. He joined in the dancing and singing with gusto. So did young Tyr Stofin Vingham, who was by way of being an apprentice in the Foreign Office trade, so to speak. And the Vallian Courier, Hikdar Naghan Veerling, proved to possess a truly fine voice.

He gave us the Canticles of the Rose City, and we sang the old songs of Kregen, and especially of Vallia, and Llando regaled us with "The Brumbyte's Love Potion." Then a calculated and diabolical plot was hatched and I heard the good folk gathered there audibly wondering just what song the emperor would choose to delight them with.

Well, now!

I can rumble out a hoarse chorus on the march, and I'll willingly join in when the swods sing—but to perform a solo under the admiring gazes of these people? I'd done it before, of course, and no doubt would again, but, all the same. . . .

In the end I chomped and chewed and spat my way through a fine rousing swordsman's song: "Kurin and the Risslaca of Fire-Cavern."

After that we sang for some long time and after that again a few of us were gathered in a comfortable nook and I showed them the golden zhantil mask I kept still in the sack in which it had been catapulted along with me by the Scorpion. We'd not had time to make golden zhantil masks for ourselves when we'd gone up and burned the

temple. I felt confident that these men, knowing of the
evil, might themselves fashion golden zhantil masks.

Then Strom Ortyg said: "I have no doubt from intelligence gathered by my agents that the army recruiting
here is bound for Tomboram. I have sent notice of that to
Strazab Larghos ti Therminsax, our ambassador in
Tomboram. Such information could prove useful to him."

"The people of Port Marsilus burned our embassy there,
and Strazab Larghos had to escape to safety, which I am
assured he did—"

"Majister!"

"Aye, Ortyg, an unpleasant business. The truth is both
armies forming here in North Pandahem are aimed at
Vallia—"

The people in that group reacted in their various ways,
from surprise and indignation, to fury and determination
to hit back.

"—and they would interfere with communications.
There's a Strom Murgon along there in Tomboram who
is in league with this Kov Colun Mogper. They are receiv-
ing their pay from some agency that, as yet, we have
failed to uncover. We will. We will. This Murgon aims to
kill his cousin, the Kov Pando, and, I guess, seize the
throne from under the flat slug of a King Nemo. Then he
and Kov Colun will be left ruling the roost. And Vallia
will once again be in flames."

"No! No!" They bristled now, alarmed and ugly with
resentment that after all we had done the stupid damned
Pandaheem insisted on fighting us.

Ortyg, as I judged, was too tough a character to look
shaken. He might be shattered within the turmoil of his
thoughts; but a diplomat he was, and with a diplomat's
habitual smile and bland words. He did allow himself to
voice the thought that would now torment him every
day.

"When will they get around to burning *my* embassy?"

I said, and not with much courtesy: "Find some agents
you can trust and who can worm out a little more than
the fellows you have so far managed. Call them spies. It
often gees them up."

Here in this building on its grounds we were sitting in
a tiny enclave that was Vallia surrounded by land that
was not. It is not a particularly enviable position to be in
when that surrounding land and its people turn nasty.

I had had personally to argue long and emphatically with the Presidio of Vallia to persuade them to sanction an embassy to Menaham in Pandahem. The Bloody Menahem were anathema to honest Vallians. But, after the death of Phu-Si-Yantong and the break-up of Empress Thyllis's crazy schemes, I'd imagined a new and brighter era was beginning. Convinced though I was that such an era was beginning, I had to face the fact that there were a few hiccoughs at the outset.

Like all this imbroglio.

Well, as you will readily perceive, what we had to do was obvious. Bloody obvious.

The trick would be in finding out how to do it.

CHAPTER EIGHTEEN

Naghan Veerling's adventure . . .

"Some people, you know, majister, really want to be slaves—well, not exactly slaves, I don't mean grakfodder—I mean—"

Hikdar Naghan Veerling stumbled to a halt occasioned not by my questioning look as by his suddenly apprehended inability to sort out his thoughts. He had been a staunch supporter when we'd cleared out the aragorn and the slavers from Vallia. He knew my views. So he was being honest and trying to put across a point of view sincerely held.

"I know what you mean, Naghan, even if you have it twisted up." I didn't laugh as we flew swiftly through thin air toward Port Marsilus. Naghan had easily been persuaded to drop me off outside the city before resuming his flight to Vallia. "Some people do seem to be born to be slaves, and cruel men and women just enslave them. But that is not the truth of their birth or inclinations. It's simply that some folk are less able to come to terms with life and need help and support. To enslave them has been the universal answer for seasons and seasons. The correct response to their plight is sympathy and then a program of education with an ibmaster."

"But, majister, surely you would agree that Opaz has fashioned some folk to lead and others to be led?"

"You can lead many people without making them slaves."

He glanced up quickly from the controls.

"Do not misunderstand me. I abhor slavery for what it does not only to the slave but to the slave masters. But I fell into the habit of debate during my time at the University of Bryvondrin. And, as I say, Opaz in his wisdom has seen fit to make some people—as you aptly put it—unable to comprehend what life can mean. They are the weak flock."

"Quite so. The abolition of slavery in Vallia will not miraculously give these bewildered people the capacity to handle the problems of living. We're working on that."

The Kregan scientific and religious mind functions in ways somewhat at a tangent if you take Earth as a norm. To their philosophies, Kregan thinkers bring the concept of mind and body as twins. All that is not corporeal is of the ib. This subsumes mind, soul, spirit. Yet the divisions are more subtle than a simple division; it is realized that, for instance, when a fellow is bashed over the head and his brains gush out they are the physical home of his ib, along with residual pathways in his body. But you can be "broken from the ib" and wander as a ghost. And, again, in various parts of Kregen entirely different philosophies struggle to understand and explain truths that—well, perhaps—mere mortal man was never meant to grasp. Perhaps. . . .

"Look," Naghan broke in. "Up ahead. Voller."

Any airboat flying over Pandahem was news.

We scanned the airy reaches ahead, the clouds low to the ground spinning away beneath and reflecting back a tumultuous glory of radiance from the suns.

I caught a quick glimpse of the voller before she flickered past an upflung pinnacle of cloud.

"D'you make her out?"

"She was gone too fast."

I frowned. "It might be—" I began.

"I always said so," quoth Naghan Veerling, and he laughed out loud. "If one travels with Dray Prescot, Emperor of Vallia, one is in for adventure—without a doubt!"

"Maybe an adventure not to our liking," I grumped.

"What Opaz wills Opaz wills."

"That's truth, by Vox! And any new vollers in Pandahem have to mean mischief."

We had flown out over the sea to avoid observation on the trip from Memguin in Menaham to Port Marsilus in Bormark of Tomboram. Maybe the fellow up front had the same idea. Moments later the voller popped out of the cloud. I stared narrowly. Then: "By Zair! She's *Golden Zhantil!*"

At once a sickening host of tormenting emotions hit

me, swarmed all over me, drained me, left me shaken
and haggard—

"Majister!"

"You will have to fly as you've never flown before,
Hikdar Naghan Veerling."

At my tone he braced up with a snap, immediately
aware that the time for this adventure he craved had
arrived.

"I hope, I am confident—hell, I pray! —that that voller
is piloted by a lady, the Lady Ros Delphor. She is very
dear to me. I would give my life for hers. If she is in
danger, trouble, under duress in that flier—"

"Majister! We will rescue her—who can stand against
Dray—"

"Plenty, Naghan, plenty. Now let's go down and see
what the position is."

As we went whistling down I had time to reflect that
my habitual regard for aliases and secrets, and the desire to protect Dayra's identity, must have an odd reper-
cussion here. Naghan might well be wondering why a
puissant emperor would be willing to give his life for
some unknown lady. Well, if he found out, he found out. I
stared ahead as the gap narrowed with the windrush
blustering past. *Golden Zhantil* leaped up to meet us.

Among the embassy guards had been three Valkan
longbowmen and they'd been blazingly anxious that I
should choose their best bow. Strom Ortyg had outfitted
me, of course, and provided me with an armory. Any
Kregan will have a plethora of weapons if he can. Each
Valkan longbowman was confident that his choice weapon
was the best. I did not wish to burden myself with three
bows, and so I'd chosen the finest and then attempted to
cheer up the other two crestfallen Valkans. Being of
Valka, they naturally called me Strom and regarded me
as pertaining especially to them.

Which was proper.

Now I lifted the bow and nocked a shaft. I had the
usual fleeting thought of regret that Seg was not here. . . .

"There is a slave woman at the controls, majister. That
is damned odd, by Vox!"

I had to control the furious burst of anger that threat-
ened to deluge me in scarlet hatred. I had to concentrate
on the loose.

Golden Zhantil turned below us. Her decks appeared

deserted, although anyone could be below. At the controls the slim figure of a woman in slave gray was partially surrounded by four hulking great Chuliks looking up at us. Their weapons were drawn.

"Bring us in sweetly, Naghan. I'll shaft two and then it's handstrokes."

"Aye!"

We plunged down.

Naghan Veerling handled his little Courier craft superbly. As we came in I leaned over the coaming and loosed twice. Each shot struck. Then I was over the side my sword in my fist slamming into the two remaining Chuliks.

I was quick, nasty and the result was very messy.

She said: "I am well aware of all your bad habits. This is one of your better habits. I approve."

Then—and, by all the Names—this should have happened before, I took her in my arms and she hugged me and so for a space neither could speak.

A footfall on the deck heralded Naghan Veerling. He'd parked the Courier flier on the deck of *Golden Zhantil*. Now he stumped up as we turned to watch him. His face was furious.

"By Vox!" he burst out. "This is terrible! What will I say? It is too much, majister! Damned unfair!"

"What . . . ?" said Dayra.

"Why," went on Naghan passionately, completely ignoring any conventions of meeting and of lahals, "I dare not tell a soul I went on an adventure with the emperor! They'll ask me: 'Wonderful, Naghan! And how did you fare?' And I'll damned-well *not* say that I did nothing! That it was all over before it had hardly begun! And me gawping from the back like a loon—"

The bubbling relief that Dayra was safe burst up inside me. I laughed. I, Dray Prescot, roared with merriment.

I spluttered and managed to get out: "You did well, Naghan—"

"Who is this young man who is disappointed he didn't give a Chulik the chance to degut him, father?"

I turned and Naghan said: "Father?"

So I made the pappattu between them, and Naghan was suitably quieted down and impressed. Dayra was a princess when she wanted to be, by Krun!

Her story was soon told. After leaving Lisa the Empoin

she'd returned to the flier. Nalfi was missing. Then, as Dayra said in a resentful tone: "I made a mess of it. That bastard Strom Murgon caught me prettily, a point at my throat and nowhere to turn. He made me fly him away. Since then he's used the voller nonstop. It is amazing how much work there is for a lone flier in this country."

"I give thanks to Opaz you are safe, Dayra."

"Oh, they didn't harm me. I could fly the voller. They couldn't. I'm on my way back from dropping a party of spies in Vallia—"

That explained why the voller was empty apart from the Chuliks set to guard her. I said: "Give Naghan all the information you can. When he reaches Vallia a party will have to pick up these spies as soon as possible."

So that was arranged.

When Naghan was ready to leave, Dayra said: "I knew a Nath Veerling once. We were in Bryvondrin at the time—"

"My twin. He is regarded by the family rather as the zorca with the splintered horn. But we got along. I have not heard from him in many seasons."*

Dayra smiled, the colour in her cheeks, her eyes bright. By Zair! She'd taken her rescue mighty coolly; but I guessed what she was feeling now. She masked all that by saying: "Yes, we had some rollicking times."

That, of course, was in Dayra's madcap days when she and her gang of cronies went around wrecking restaurants for fun. Out of that had grown the darker evils of Zankov.

Hikdar Naghan Veerling, a Courier for Vallia, lifted away.

"Remberee, Naghan!"

"Remberee, princess, majister."

We were left on the deck, Dayra and I, and I could feel a warming of my blood, a treacherous feeling of contentment. There was so much to do, by Krun, and yet the clouds about us seemed to me to take on a roseate tinge.

Now with Dayra safe, surely we would win through!

* Equates with "The black sheep of the family."—A.B.A.

CHAPTER NINETEEN

Duurn the Doomsayer

He brushed up his reddish whiskers under that smart foxy nose and his bright eyes appeared almost crossed, so shrewd were they.

"If we steal away the treasure again—which we could do, by Horato the Potent, which we could do! —that misbegotten, white-haired she-witch will melt it all back."

"Let us take the treasure, anyway; then, by the oozing sores and desiccating limbs of the Divine Lady of Belschutz, if the witch does, she does."

Other voices lifted in passionate argument, each demanding to go down and seize Strom Murgon's treasure and let that damned frizzle-haired witch try to do her worst.

We were all sitting or lounging in the main saloon of the voller *Golden Zhantil*. After that beautiful reunion with Dayra, I had instead of going on to Port Marsilus, flown to seek out Pompino and our comrades, finding them marching not particularly happily down the trails to reach civilization. They were overjoyed to see Dayra and me—and, I truly think, far more in *Golden Zhantil*. These Pandaheem were very rapidly acquiring the taste for flying.

As I saw it, this particular situation was both comical and alarming.

I had to prevent that army sailing to Vallia. We had already taken the army's treasury, and that damned witch had retaken it. If we just swingled in again to repeat the process, would the lady-necromancer not do the same?

When we had chance for a private conversation, Pompino, with natural quick eagerness, wanted to know

what the hell had happened to me when the Everoinye
snatched me away.

"They left me behind, Jak. Ignored me. They chose
you—"

"Only because I was there and you had gone back to
the campfires. If I had gone, you would have been chosen."

"You think so?"

"I'm certain sure."

"Hmph," he sniffed. "Well, and what happened?"

A considerable degree of caution had to be employed in
my recital. He'd be vastly energized to discover just how
I'd inveigled a party of soldiers from the Vallian Embassy to assist me. So, I confess, it seemed like boasting
when I ran it all together and rescued Carrie and burned
the Lemmite temple all in one coup de main. One day, I
supposed unhappily, Pompino would have to know I was
this puissant and frustrated Emperor of Vallia. Then
he'd change. Then I might lose a comrade.

Pompino possessed this exaggerated respect for the
Star Lords that would, inevitably, spill over into his
dealings with emperors and kings. Even so, even so, he
was well up to liberating an emperor's property if the
chance came . . .

"We will have to find another way of stopping the
army," I said to Dayra when we, in our turn, had the
chance for further private conversation. "Pompino and
the lads would go for the treasure again; but that, I am
convinced, would be merely a waste of time. And they
would think twice—even those hairy rascals—of taking
on the entire army to strike at supporters of Lem the
Silver Leem. It's not so much a puzzle of what must quite
clearly be done—"

"That's obvious, father."

"Quite so. But the doing of it will upset a number of
people." I looked at my daughter. "It will not please me,
Ros Delphor, and can you understand that?"

"You are just an old romantic."

"True."

"Although I wonder which will displease you most; the
cause or the effect?"

"The cause will be objects, the effects people."

"And in this wicked world that does not answer the
question!"

And, by Zair, she was right.

"We will have to contrive some excuse to get the lads off the voller. All of them, without exception, have no reason to prevent an attack on Vallia." I sounded sad and tired even in my own ears. "On the contrary. Despite all we in Vallia have done to create friendships with them here in Pandahem, they'll approve of an attack on us."

"Even Pompino?"

"Of course. He's a good Pandaheem, from the South, maybe, like most of them. But I'll wager young Pando would rejoice to go and swing a sword in our land. Despite all."

"Then," she said, and her lovely mouth tightened into a resolute bar. "They must be taught differently."

I did not reply to that. Dayra was still very much of an enigma to me, to my sorrow. Any sensible father takes an intense interest in all the doings of his daughters; but he does not pry. He worries his guts out over them; but they go their own way. I was not fool enough to make a stupid blunt inquiry as to Dayra's feelings for Pando. I had the strongest hunch that that young man would not measure up to what Dayra fancied she wanted, and I also felt even more strongly that Dayra would remain free from emotional entanglements for some considerable time. She wouldn't even think of marrying yet; she might never marry.

But she'd have a damned good time, all the same.

As a part of those thoughts, I spoke as though musing aloud.

"I hope Hyr Brun is well and safe. And the child, also, Vaxnik—"

"He is a child no longer! He is a fair limber young man—"

"I believe it, and with joy. He and Hyr Brun—they served you well."

And still I would not pry. The central aching question could not be asked.

Dayra said: "I do not think you realize how much we missed you when we were young, Jaidur and I. We knew only that we had a father who was nowhere. We didn't miss *you*—we lacked a father. Jaidur said he would call himself Vax and seek adventure. You know that my idea of adventure was—somewhat different—"

"Aye." I wanted to listen, silent and fascinated by

these revelations. But I said, "Jaidur went out to the Eye
of the World, became a Krozair, called himself Vax
Neemusjid. And you smashed up honest folk's restaurants—"

She made a small dismissing motion. "One of my clos-
est friends was Patti na—" She stopped herself. Then:
"Never mind her real name. I thought she and Jaidur
would—but they did not. Patti married the one we called
Vondo. They were both slain in an affray. And so I
became responsible for their son, Vondonik, and called
him Vaxnik."

Did I feel a deliquescence of hope? Was I pleased or
disappointed? I did not know. I waited in silence.

She half-turned, not laughing; but bright, bright, the
old memories stirring her. "You will have to wait to hear
of Hyr Brun for here comes Pando. And he concerns us
here and now much more than—"

"Hai!" called Pando as he advanced across the deck of
Golden Zhantil. "Here you are! I have made up my mind.
I have waited too long. I am going to teach my cousin
Strom Murgon a lesson he will not forget. The final
lesson."

Pando became very much the fire-eating young noble,
a gallant kov determined to strike for what was right-
fully his. No more hesitation, he said, and issued orders
left, right and center.

The nub of the scheme was to destroy, banish or capture Strom Murgon.

Pando was not fussy which one it happened to be,
although in private bets we tended to favor the first
solution as the one most pleasing to young Kov Pando.

Although, after we touched down in a forest camp set
up some miles inland of Port Marsilus, as Pompino con-
fided in me: "Your young friend Pando doesn't appear to
have any really sound plan of operations."

"Don't underestimate him, Pompino. You know how
these young bloods are when they have had a taste of
power and it has been dashed from them. Anyway, the
nub of his plan is the Ifts. Twayne Gullik has at last
declared openly for Kov Pando his master and has, at
last, brought in the Forest Ifts actively to assist."

"Oh, yes, I know all that. Gullik was his usual supercilious smirking self when he rode in. And they intend to
use the secret way into the Zhantil Palace."

That was the tortuous secret passageway system we had used under Mindi the Mad's direction to escape. A crowd of warriors pressing in through there could well take the palace, particularly, if . . . "And we drop in from above in *Golden Zhantil!*"

"Aye."

"It is after that. Pando will hold the palace, and this time the army with Murgon will be actively hostile. He cannot resist for long. Then what?"

"I tend to the opinion," I said, a trifle cautiously, "that Pando hopes to have finished with Murgon by then."

"He'll need to be slippy. That one is a sly customer, and cunningly tough with it."

"It is my view, and I regret the necessity although joying in the venture, that I will have to lie to Pando." I added quickly, "Oh, not actively lie. I'll lie, as it were, in absentia. It won't be a personal falsehood."

"Do what?"

"You'll see."

He grumped off then to see about the next meal, and I sought out Dayra, who must be a party to the scheme.

She fired up at once, and made all the preparations.

So it was that toward the rise of She of the Veils, ever, I believe, my favorite Moon of Kregen, a grotesque figure shambled into the camp among the trees.

Cap'n Murkizon and Nath Kemchug led him forward into the firelight. Then they moved away, out of smelling range.

Grotesque, that figure, aye, and weird. His heavy beard was checkered into red and blue, and likewise his whiskers. His hair stuck up in spikes, colored yellow and orange and blue. His face was streaked with indigo and vermilion. His eyes glared frightfully. He was clad in a mangy animal hide of uncertain parentage, cinctured by a belt of monkey's paws, fastened by a bronze clasp in the form of an apim skull.

At his side swung a pallixter, a heavy knife snugged in a sheath over his hip, and he leaned on a mighty staff of twisted wood, the convoluted root of balass, black and grained, festooned with small evil-smelling bags, and tintinnambulating with a myriad tiny bells.

Men and women shrank away from that uncouth figure. He breathed an aura of mystery and repellent blasphemy.

"Llahal and Lahal!" he called in a strident, nerve-sawing

voice. He moved with a heaviness and a hint of unsteadiness. He advanced toward the fire, and halted, and spread his arms wide, and then thumped the great staff down so that all the bells danced and clamored.

"I am Duurn the Doomsayer!"

Pando and Pompino stepped up, shoulder to shoulder, not one whit discomfitted, although Twayne Gullik hung back well to the rear, and the guard Fristles congregated on the far side of the fire. Cap'n Murkizon gripped his axe and stood four square. Larghos the Flatch, who was not himself since the loss of the lady Nalfi, stood at Murkizon's side, lowering and hating. Rondas the Bold, just about recovered from his wound, stood with them, ready and alert.

"Lahal, Duurn the Doomsayer," quoth Pando. "And what is it you want with us? Whose doom do you say?"

"The doom of all in Bormark, all in Tomboram!"

A gasp went up at this. No one seemed to know if they should scoff at this weird, or freeze with fear.

"A mighty army marches on Bormark. They come like the sands of the seashore, marching from Memguin, out of Menaham. They march with a golden glittering lord at their head. They come to destroy all who oppose them and seize your steadings, your wealth, your women—"

Pando believed this at once.

Pompino said: "And how, mighty warlock, do you know this?"

I was highly amused at the look this Duurn the Doomsayer bestowed on my comrade.

"Unbeliever! Blasphemer! What know you of the Arts! Tremble lest your impiety bring you low!"

And, then: "I saw the host, marching."

At that, Pando shot out: "How many? What forces? Their captains? Their rate of march? Their order? Tell me all you can, Duurn the Doomsayer, and you may name your price."

"There is no price in all Bormark that could rise to my just desserts! For I have the Eye! I have the Ear! I can scry past the mundane veils of the known! Beware lest idle curiosity burn you up as the moth is consumed by the candle."

Dayra moved with all the grace of a hunting cat leaping after her prey. She slid in from the side, quick and deadly, while Duurn the Doomsayer began to thunder more rhetorical outpourings extolling his sorcerous powers; Dayra, passing by, halted momentarily, then went on past the firelight.

In that slight pause, as she passed, she whispered: "You're overdoing it, father!"

So, incontinently, vanquished by common sense, Duurn the Doomsayer thundered his last dire doom saying, and turned away and stumped off, out of the firelight, back into the forest.

CHAPTER TWENTY

How lord and lady
cried their Remberees

So the great plan of Pando's went into operation.

Twayne Gullik together with a host of his Ifts and a sizeable force of men still loyal to the Kov of Bormark, entered the secret passageway and penetrated into the Zhantil Palace through the hidden corridors. We, for our part, flew down in *Golden Zhantil* bristling with weaponry.

The attacks were timed to coincide a full four glasses after the rising of the Maiden with the Many Smiles. We hoped to have the palace cleared by dawn.

In the fuzzy pink moonshine we soared down and leaped from the voller, teeth bared, weapons sharp, raging to get into action.

I'd been spoiled for choice in the matter of weapons. The only real lack was a Krozair longsword. Still, the drexer gladly given me by Strom Ortyg served supremely well. I had the Valkan longbow. And I had repossessed the rapier and main gauche kept by Pompino when I'd been hoicked up by the Everoinye. We went howling in like a pack of wild beasts.

With the twin onslaught the defenders of the palace crumbled and broke. That furious assault smashed them, drove them like chaff, swept them up as a slave girl sweeps up the dust of the lord's Great Hall.

Panting, flushed, triumphant, we broke the last of Murgon's mercenaries as they attempted a stand, according to their lights, swirling in headlong combat down the grand staircase and along the luxurious halls and corridors. They could not stand before us.

Like good quality Kregan paktuns who earn their hire in blood, they fought well. There was no quailing, no shrieking panic flight; these men and women had taken their pay and now they earned their hire. In honor, when

158

the situation cleared unmistakably and the steel-bokkertu could be offered and made—why then, and only then, would these paktuns change their allegiances.

As usual I was most anxious to get all this nasty fighting business over and done with as soon as possible. Pando, exalted, a single trembling entity on the point of explosion, took some time before he set the steel-bokkertu in motion. By then, more men and women had died earning their hire.

Fragments of poetry echoed along in my skull; and I am sure, Kregen being Kregen, many a savage fighting warrior—female or male—kept up a ragged rhythm of swing and strike as the stanzas seethed in their brains. Poetry and death—ever the two are twinned. . . .

"Do not, my heart, get your fool self killed at the last moment—"

"I shall not hang back in dishonor, you great dear buffoon—"

Quendur and Lisa, striking blow for blow, were at their accustomed arguments.

Poor Larghos the Flatch watched them in hopeless envy.

The Divine Lady of Belschutz entered the conversation from time to time, fruitily.

Rondas the Bold wished to take out some repayment for his wound. Nath Kemchug, like any Chulik, sowed death in his wake. As usual when divorced from their beloved varters, Wilma the Shot and Alwim the Eye shot in their bows with deft precision. Naghan the Pellendur, recently appointed shal-cadade,* led his Fristle guards with our onslaught. The cadade, Framco the Tranzer, had been assigned the secret entrance and this, I felt, was as much because Pando wished to keep an eye on Twayne Gullik. Mantig the Screw distinguished himself during that fight. Jespar the Scundle was not with us—he had thankfully returned to his own people.

"I," said Dayra to me as we cleared one of the ornate chambers leading onto the hallway below the grand staircase, "abhor killing people unnecessarily. Why doesn't this young onker Pando negotiate? We have clearly won.

---

* Shal-cadade—Under (or vice-) captain of the guard. From the root word "umshal" meaning shadow. The shal-cadade stands in the shadow of the cadade, a neat conceit.—A.B.A.

Is there no one with enough authority over him to make
him see sense and initiate the steel-bokkertu with the
surviving paktuns?"

Dayra halted stubbornly at the entrance to the chamber and stared malevolently out onto the hall where the
foot of the grand staircase swept out into a recurve.
Statues decorated every other tread of the staircase, and
the high balcony above was just visible from where we
stood. She shook her head. "The get onker!"

"We keep referring to Pando as young Pando," I said,
and I, too, stopped beside the entrance and looked out
onto the last dying flickers of the combat. "But he is not
so young these days. Like any hot-blooded lord he is
difficult to control. And, it is perfectly clear, he will not
desist from this fight until Murgon—"

"Ah! Malignant, then—"

"Not really." I'd given Dayra most of my past history
in connection with Pando and his mother, Tilda the Fair,
Tilda of the Many Veils. She did understand, of course;
but like me the sight of wanton slaughter filled her with
revulsion.

The stink of spilled blood, the feel of sweat in the air,
the harshness of all this, gave us pause, there in the
doorway of the hall with the grand staircase lofting above.

Dayra had not worn her Claw in this fight.

A Sister of the Rose normally keeps her Claw in its
bronze or silver-bound balass box, secret. But that box
would be an awkward encumbrance to a girl in a fight
before she dons the Claw, and so usually the talons are
secreted in a leather and canvas bag which can be slung
on her back out of the way. These bags normally are
quite plain, perhaps with a row of fancy red stitching to
distinguish them one from another. The Claw itself will
have each separate tooth masked by a sheath of ivory or
bone, or perhaps of wood. Now, through the insights
afforded me by the Everoinye, I happened to know that
these sacks are called jikvarpams.

In the fight Dayra had used thraxter and shield.

She had also been armored.

I own I'd raised my voice a trifle when we'd been
equipping ourselves before the off. I'd been insistent.
She'd said, with a toss of her head, words more or less to
the effect that if I wanted to make a scene then she'd
damned well wear armor, and carry a shield. I'd replied

that I'd make more than a scene if she got herself killed.
We were, you will perceive, improving in our relationship.

Now she reached around and fretfully began to pluck
at the jikvarpam on her back, the blood from her thraxter
staining the canvas.

"Where is Pando, or Murgon? By Vox! I need a wet!"

"By who?"

She glared at me.

"By Chusto, then, you—you—"

Dayra, like all my children, knew how to use a sword
and shield with superb skill, having been trained by
Balass the Hawk. She slid the shield off her left arm, and
dumped it against the door jamb. She looked pretty
ferocious, I can tell you.

A step at our backs brought me around sharpish. I
relaxed. The Lady Dafni walked up. She wore a middle-
length white gown, belted in gold, and there were flowers in her hair. Her face was composed, yet I detected an
overbrightness there, a quivering sense of panic sup-
pressed by sheer self-preservation. Odd.

Pando walked with her, dignified and warlike in armor,
carrying a naked sword. With them among the retainers
came the Mytham twins, Pynsi and Poldo. Both were
outfitted for battle, both carried bows.

Pando did not look pleased.

"We have gained the day," he said, surly and vengeful.
"But where is the rast Murgon? He hides away like a
skulking pest of the sewers. Jikarna, I brand him,
jikarna!"*

"Not so!" The lady Dafni pointed aloft. "Look!"

Up there on the head of the grand staircase a brisk
little fight finished with a couple of Rapas falling, and
Strom Murgon, blood-bespattered, flushed, waving his
sword in contempt at us clustered below.

Pando rushed out to get a better view, yelling that the
cramph would escape. We followed.

Murgon brandished his blood-befouled sword at us. He
looked magnificent, filled with elan and fighting spirit,
defying us to the death.

Poldo Mytham did not hesitate.

He lifted his bow and on his face the shattering hatred
filling him rendered him demonic. He loosed.

* Jikarna—coward.

The shaft struck Murgon in the neck, above the corselet rim.

He stood for a moment, surprised.

He dropped his sword. He swayed. Then he pitched over the railing and fell headlong to the polished marble below.

Poldo lowered his bow. He loved Dafni with a hopeless longing. Perhaps he thought. . . . Well, who knows what he thought?

With a horrified shriek, Dafni rushed forward. In a smother of white dress she collapsed onto her knees beside Murgon. His head was a ghastly red pudding. She took that hideous object in her arms and rested it in her lap and bent over him, her face stained with his blood as she kissed that crushed and ghastly face. She crooned hysterical words . . .

"Murgon! My only true love—my heart—*Murgon!*"

"So," said Dayra softly, at my side, "so that was the way of it. It explains much."

"Aye."

From somewhere in the shadows—and to this day neither I nor anyone else knows who loosed—a crossbow bolt lanced the air, thudding into Dafni, smashing her forward. She collapsed over the shattered body of her lover. Together, blood mingling with blood, they lay in death.

No one spoke.

The part Dafni had played in this business now appeared plain. She and Murgon had loved each other—and in furtherance of his plans he had used her to bedazzle Pando. The interview I had witnessed was now explained, and when we'd rescued Dafni—she had not wanted to be rescued. Pando had been the victim all along. Tilda of the Many Veils had seen much; but her intoxication as a way of life had precluded any clear statements to aid us. And the Mytham twins?

Poldo was distraught. And Pynsi—would she now be able to marry Pando? Only the future could answer that.

The immediate task was to ensure the loyalty of Pando's people, and the army waiting outside Port Marsilus. Into that hush the sound of a man yelling in pain penetrated and Pompino appeared, brisk and bright and most foxy, dragging along a wight by one ear.

"Says he has a message for Strom Murgon which, I think, with a little persuasion, he might tell us!"

Pompino halted as he saw the two bodies, blood-befouled, sprawled together. He whistled.

"That takes care of *that*, then!"

The order of events had to be kept in a correct sequence. The cadade and his Fristle guards went off to secure the palace. Palace slaves and servants set about clearing away the detritus of battle—which is a way of saying that they collected up the corpses. Pando shouted passionately that they should treat Dafni with care and that she should be laid out in state in a bedroom. As for Murgon; he turned away and it was clear to us all that he didn't give a damn if they bunged Murgon's corpse on the dung heap.

Dayra went off to make sure that that didn't happen. At least she knew how to treat a beaten adversary.

In all this bustle Pompino's capture stood sullenly waiting to be questioned. He was a Brokelsh, hairy and uncouth, and one eye was black and his face was cut.

I looked at Pando curious to know how he would react to the knowledge that Dafni had been beguiling him all the time, under orders from Murgon to secure Murgon's desires to control the kovnate. For all her ceaseless chatter, Dafni proved herself to have been a lady of spirit.

Pando just pushed all that aside. His choleric noble attitude just brushed away the implications. He rounded on Pompino. "Well, Khibil! Don't just stand there! What is the message this rast has for Murgon?"

Pompino twisted a red whisker, and most mildly said: "Speak up, Bargal the Ley. Strom Murgon is dead and Kov Pando is your liege lord."

"Yes, well—" began this Bargal the Ley, mumbling.

Pando roared: "Speak up or your hide will decorate the battlements!"

"Message from Kov Colun Mogper of Mursham, pantor!"

Dayra appeared at my side, silently, like a jungle predator. She touched me lightly on the arm.

"Oh? Yes?" bellowed Pando, incensed. "And?"

"He is ready for the great expedition against Vallia, pantor! He awaits word from you to finalize the date! Send me back with this information and the two fleets can sail."

"There is treachery here." Pando fairly snarled in his bewilderment. "Mogper advances to attack Bormark!"

"Your pardon, pantor!" No one contradicts a great lord when he is incensed without peril. "Not so! The kov is in alliance with Bormark. The venture is against Vallia."

His brows fairly writhing in indecision, Pando half-turned to look at us, all standing in a half-circle and watching in fascination. "That is certainly what I believed. That bastard Murgon at least had that right. But the grotesque, Duurn the Doomsayer—could he have been mistaken?"

Taking this as a direct question, everyone started off on a passionate braying of their own beliefs. Dayra and I remained quiet. I glanced at her.

The rustic hermit she'd found in the woods and from whom she'd borrowed the trappings of Duurn the Doomsayer had been rewarded with a handful of gold and seen safely on his way. As a powerful inducement to belief, the guise of the grotesque had seemed to me to be excellent. Not many other visitors could, I thought, have impressed Pando so strongly. But—was all that skill and artifice to go for nothing?

Then Pompino—my good comrade, my kregoinye companion, Scauro Pompino the Iarvin, stepped out and spoke.

"I believe what this messenger, Bargal the Ley, says. The army here and in Menaham is paid for in gold that can only be used for that purpose for which it was intended. Pay the army from Murgon's treasury. Set them forward in the venture against Vallia. For, kov, if you leave them idle around here they will prove a permanent and costly threat."

"Aye," rumbled Pando. "That is sooth."

At my side, Dayra whispered: "Nice friends you have."

"Pompino is a Pandaheem. He is right. If the army out there contains very many officers loyal to Murgon they can walk in here and we'll never stop 'em. Pando's best bet is to pay 'em and ship 'em out—"

"Out—against Vallia!"

"Aye."

"So much for your wonderful Duurn the Doomsayer!"

The movement among the throng indicated that Pando had made up his mind. Murgon's treasure would be distributed to the army and the ship-masters. The armada would sail for Vallia. Win or lose for that army, Pando would come out ahead.

I looked out over that bright and busy bustle as folk ran to do Kov Pando's bidding. Oh, yes, he'd come out all right, sweet and smelling of violets. But what of the country that was my home, what of Vallia?

"Very well," I said, and although Dayra listened, I was really speaking to myself. "Sink me! If it's got to be done it's got to be done. And let Opaz take care of my conscience."

CHAPTER TWENTY-ONE

Of one broken leg

Having made up his mind, Pando was all blaze and eagerness to get the thing done and over with.

Murgon's treasure—that same hoard of wealth we in *Tuscurs Maiden* had seen melt and run fuming into the sea—being distributed to the army and the ship masters delighted all of them. There was no talk anywhere of pulling down Kov Pando in the name of the dead Strom Murgon. Kovs, after all, are kovs.

Pompino and the crew went about looking over their shoulders in momentary expectation of the ghastly apparition of the white-haired witch. Had she turned up and blasted us all no one would have been vastly surprised.

From a dusty and hidden portion of the palace a figure that was surprising emerged, blinking in the suns' radiance. Cap'n Murkizon, axe aslant, sent immediately for Larghos the Flatch.

Stumbling, her clothes in ruins, her face streaked with dirt and tears, the Lady Nalfi was caught up and clasped close to Larghos. He could hardly believe his good fortune.

We left them to their reunions, and later Larghos and Nalfi joined us where she was able to tell her story.

Dayra watched, a comically quizzical little frown denting in between her eyebrows.

We gathered in a little outdoor arbor furnished with cane chairs and striped awnings and wobbly-legged tables. In a siege the place could be converted to take a catapult. Nalfi professed to bewilderment, loss of memory, misery, fear. Yes, she remembered the flying boat and watching Lisa and Ros Delphor leaving her alone. She had been terrified.

Here Dayra pursed up her lips.

Nalfi had hidden somewhere within the voller and

only hunger had been enough to conquer her terror. She
had crept out to find herself back in the Zhantil Palace,
and had somehow slunk out of the airboat and found a
succession of hiding places. That part was easy enough to
believe, on Kregen where most of the palaces are stuffed
to bursting with slaves and retainers and very few people know all the souls under the same roof.

Pompino expressed our general pleasure at seeing the
Lady Nalfi alive and well. He congratulated her on her
courage in adversity.

Dayra said to me, sotto voce, "Huh!"

"It is true, though. Nalfi possesses great courage, and
resourcefulness."

Dayra glanced at me as though I had straw sticking
out of my hair.

Looking out over the sea the eye was caught instantly
by the assemblage of shipping. Seabirds wheeled and
cawed amid the forest of masts. Nalfi expressed herself
as most pleased that Menaham and Tomboram were co-
operating. For two countries of Pandahem to act in this
way was a fine augury for the future. I'd have been more
inclined to agree with these pious sentiments had the
target of the cooperation not been my home of Vallia.

The departure of the fleet could not now be long delayed.
To no one's surprise, Pompino and the crew decided to
sign on for the expedition. As Pompino said, twirling up
his right whisker and gripping his sword hilt with his
left fist: "Those rasts of Vallians are bound to worship
Lem and their evil land be teeming with temples to burn."

Dayra said, a trifle too sharply, "The cult of Lem was
once brought to Vallia. I hear the emperor was most
severe with them—"

"I wonder," sniffed Pompino. Then: "This is sooth?"

"So I heard."

Making some excuse I managed to drag Dayra off. We
spoke alone out on the battlements.

"All right, father—I know!"

"Forget that. We have to try something interesting
before . . . Duurn the Doomsayer failed. I think we have a
more sure tool to our hands."

She was a true daughter to Delia, Empress of Vallia.
Quick, by Zair! Sharp and devious and intelligent and
altogether lovely. "Yes. You have seen how Larghos the

Flatch goes about these days since Nalfi returned? Like a puppy that has lost his favorite chewing slipper."

"You were quite right when you said she had no affection for him. I think that was the key that unlocked the rest of it for me."

We had regaled Dayra with the tale of how Nalfi had joined our company back in Peminswopt along the coast. We'd cleared out the Devil's Academy where they trained up the priests to torture and butcher children to the greater glory of Lem, and Nalfi, all naked and alone and held captive by a Chulik, had calmly taken his dagger from his belt and slit his throat. He had been standing in front of her, ready to fight Larghos and Cap'n Murkizon as they broke in. Dayra saw.

"So she slew the Chulik who was trying to protect her."

"What better recommendation?"

"So she's a Brown and Silver, then."

"A most courageous and resourceful Lemmite, as I said. She saw she'd be for the chop; she joined us and ever since has been a spy in our midst. When we rescued Dafni—Murgon knew. Nalfi was missing, and joined us with some excuse—and more than once."

"And the scrap of brown and silver ribbon that would have betrayed our escape, down in the sewers—"

"As I said. Courageous and resourceful."

"Maybe I should have a word with her with my Claw."

"Perhaps over the matter of Larghos, at some later time. Right now, Dayra my tiger-girl, we must go in for some theater."

I admit it with great pleasure—we arranged this little piece of live theater exquisitely.

Fortune favored us to the extent that Larghos and Nalfi indulged in a real row in a small room, almost a broom cupboard, off the snug withdrawing chamber where Dayra and I sat. They exchanged wearily familiar accusations and disclaimers. The truth is, like marital infidelities, one side seems to wander around as though struck blind. Larghos stormed off in the opposite direction without seeing us, and before Nalfi could follow, Dayra spoke up in her clear voice.

"I feel for poor Larghos; but he will cheer up wonderfully when we reach Menaham. When he takes his part

in the sack of Memguin—and that's just for starters!
—he'll have so much gold—"

"Ros Delphor! Careful! You speak of secrets, and you
do not know who may be listening."

"No one. They've gone." She laughed in a conspirato-
rial way, almost giggling. "Because you knew Kov Pando
when he was a young boy means he trusts you above
many others. I think his scheme to gull Kov Colun Mogper
with messages that we sail to Vallia, and then to march
straight to Memguin and seize the place when Mogper is
away—"

"Oh, yes, Pando is mighty clever. Colun Mogper will
suspect nothing. His army will be cut up in that heathen
Vallia, and probably never return, and we'll be busily
burning temples to Lem the Silver Leem. Any Lemmites
left are likely to find themselves in small pieces. Very
small."

"Like the pieces of their sacrifices."

A tiny, birdlike sound from the smaller room. . . .

Dayra said, "I am for a wet, Jak Leemsjid."

"And I am with you, Ros Delphor."

Later on Twayne Gullik, the castellan of the Zhantil
Palace, reported in great annoyance that some cramph or
cramphs had stolen two zorcas. Fine animals, they were
worth much gold. If food had been stolen, as it would
have been, by Vox! then it would not be missed among
the mounds of forage produced at all hours in the kitchens.

Dayra told me with great satisfaction: "She's well on
her way to Memguin to report the terrible news to
Mogper."

"May he have joy of it, by Zair!"

"Being what he is, he'll start at once his riposte."

"We have to move before they start loading the ships
here. I've organized Naghan Raerdu, our local Vallian
agent—"

"Naghan the Barrel, the Nose, the Ale! I know him!"

I sighed. "He is a most remarkable and trustworthy
man. He made it possible for me to penetrate the Lemmite
temple, where we met—"

"Hanging in bonds on the wall and that rast Zankov—"

"That is past. We look to the future."

"Aye, by Chusto!"

Naghan Raerdu, a most adroit spy within the emperor's
private apparat, spluttered and wheezed and laughed his

way into providing all we required. He employed tools who, I am sure, had no idea they worked for Vallia.

"Why, majister," he choked, laughing, his face as scarlet as the radiance of Zim, his eyes shut and streaming happy tears. "These poor folk of Pandahem cannot tell one airboat from another. The work will be finished before the Suns set, aye, and the paint dry!"

He was right. If you do not understand aircraft you're not likely to spot the difference between a Bf109 and a Mustang when there is only the flick of a wing to see. If you don't understand ships you will not spot the subtle differences between the t'gallants of a Johnny Crapaud Seventy-four from a British Seventy-four, pitching off there just above the horizon rim.

Naghan Raerdu had the work completed in a clearing in the forest at a distance removed from Port Marsilus. He ensured there were no nosey Ifts about. His people splashed on the blue and green paint, rigged awnings, fabricated the many flags. These treshes were all the same; blue and green diagonal stripes separated by narrow strips of white. This was the flag of Menaham.

When Naghan Raerdu said what I expected him to say, I replied: "No, Naghan. Absolutely no."

"But majister! Princess—I appeal to you—"

"Look, my friend. As a purveyor of best ale, as the emperor's most valued secret agent, you are far too valuable where you are, doing what you do. If you risk your neck with us—"

"Majister! If I thought there was a risk, well, I am not sure I could agree to you both going. Also, I would not be very keen to go myself. . . ."

Dayra laughed delightedly. Even I smiled.

Naghan Raerdu, as a Vallian spy in a hostile land, ran his neck into plenty of risks every day.

He fussily superintended the stowage of the earthenware pots, making sure they were well packed down in straw. His cover as an ale merchant well qualified him for this task.

Despite all the jollity and the coarse remarks, I was decidedly unhappy about what we set out to do. Of course, it was obvious. Painfully obvious. All the same, much of the pain was experienced by me, for, do not forget, I am a plain sailorman. I do not profess to be an honest sailorman, by Zair; but this destruction saddened me.

Well, they say men sow corn for Zair to sickle.

We stood, Dayra and I, to watch Naghan Raerdu and his people ride off aboard their lumbering wagons, pulled by patient Quoffas like perambulating hearthrugs. For a treacherous moment we waited as the last wagon vanished into the surrounding forest. We were very late. From the opposite direction a scurry of zorca-mounted warriors broke from the screen of trees. They hared for us as we stood like a pair of loons on the grass, the mass of the voller at our backs.

We heard their war cries as they charged.

"Rasts of Lemmites!" And: "Charge, for the Golden Zhantil!"

Each warrior wore a golden zhantil mask.

"By the disgusting suppurating eyeballs and putrescent fingernails of Makki Grodno!" I yelled. "Up with you, my girl!"

Dayra sprang for the voller and began to clamber aloft to reach the controls. I stepped onto the fighting gallery and turned, watching the rush. One man led out, whirling his sword, low over his zorca's neck. The airboat did not move. The zorca fleeted nearer.

The leader outdistanced the rest of his cutthroat gang. He roared in, the zorca a splendid sight, all flashing hooves and wild eyes and tossing horn.

The voller moved. She shifted from the grass and lifted a handsbreadth. I let out a sigh, knowing that in the next instant Dayra would slam over the controls to full lift and we'd skyrocket aloft.

In that instant this ferocious warrior in the glittering golden mask leaped from his zorca. He hurled straight at the fighting gallery below the airboat. His clutching fingers scrabbled, caught a purchase and as we went whisking aloft so he flopped over and dangled by one hand, suspended over thin air.

I had no quarrel with him. I could not let him fall to his death. His companions were left far below, dwindling dots in the clearing, brandishing their swords. I looked down.

The voice within the golden mask puffed out, muffled.

"Jak! Jak Leemsjid, you great fambly! What are you playing at? Haul me aboard, for the sweet sake of Horato the Potent!"

I jumped forward, grabbed Pompino by the wrist and

hauled him inboard, all tumbled in his war harness along the fighting gallery. His head clanked into a straw-stuffed box filled with pots. He sat up, ripped the mask off, and glared at me, filled with fury, reddish whiskers bristling.

"What the hell are you playing at, Jak!"

"And what the hell d'you think you're doing?"

He sat up and rubbed his head. "Mindi the Mad scryed out and managed to tell us a mysterious airboat skulked in a clearing in the forest. But you—what's going on?"

"Damned half-Ift witches!" I said, most grumpily.

"Well—and what is it, Jak. Tell me!"

This, as you will readily perceive, was not part of the careful plans at all. Not at all. . . .

The voller lifted and turned and steered for Port Marsilus.

I eyed Pompino. He looked bewildered and wild. At least he'd lost his thraxter; but a rapier and left-hand dagger swung at his belts. I took a breath.

"You always were a mysterious fellow, Jak." He began to gather himself. He shook his head, and rubbed it again. "Boxes of pots—and I know little of airboats; but this looks remarkably like *Golden Zhantil*. Have you—?"

I said, "Look down there, Pompino the Iarvin."

"Do what?"

I pointed down, over the side. He turned around and leaned out to look down and I put my thumb under his ear and he went to sleep. I caught him as he fell and eased him to the deck of the fighting gallery. What a mess!

When he was thoroughly tied up and unable to move, I went up to see Dayra and told her. She looked cross.

"He would have to come poking his clever Khibil nose—"

"Yes. Well, he will not stop us."

"Of course not!"

The blue and green voller bore on, flaunting the flags of Menaham. She roared on over the forest and out over Port Marsilus as the suns declined in the bright sky. Down below, crowding the roads, tied up to every wharf, the ships of the invasion fleet lay. First thing in the morning they'd begin loading. Some of the troops would go aboard before dawn.

That armada could not be allowed to land in Vallia.

Dayra spoke and I saw she spoke diffidently. "Father—do you want to fly the voller? Would you like me to go below and—"

"Thank you, Dayra. No. I abhor this, but I'll do it."

"Very well. I'll cover every last one."

"I won't miss."

So, down below I went, back to the fighting gallery below the keel of *Golden Zhantil*. Pompino had been tied up so that he couldn't move, as I thought. He was a crafty, great-hearted, fighting Khibil. He'd wriggled himself into a position from which he could look down through a grating.

I said nothing, ignoring him. I took a torch from its becket and set it afire with flint and steel. He looked on and his Khibil face drew down.

"Jak! What—?"

I had to say out of compassion—for myself, mark it, for myself! —and not very prettily: "This had to be done."

I set the first firepot ablaze and poised with it in my hand. Pompino looked from that horrendous incendiary device down to the glinting sea. He writhed and stared back at me.

"*Tuscurs Maiden* is down there, Jak! *My* ship! A vessel you have sailed in and loved, as anyone could see. Jak! You would not burn *Tuscurs Maiden*!"

"And perhaps you should not have told Captain Linson to offer your ship to Kov Pando for his fleet."

I hurled the firepot down.

As we passed above and the next firepot hurtled down *Tuscurs Maiden* was well ablaze.

Well, I, Dray Prescot, sailorman, cannot coldly chronicle the burning of that magnificent fleet. The ships burned. The ships burned. . . .

I'd burned ships before; the *Eye of the World* had witnessed a burning. Many enemies had perished in flames of my setting. But this—no, I cannot draw that horrendous picture for you. I threw the firepots and there was a red blaze before my face and a scarlet haze in my eyes. The smoke, black and evil, drifted off before the wind.

I did not miss a single ship.

That once-proud armada sank in rinds of grimy ashes.

Long and long afterwards I learned to my great joy that not a single sailor was lost, and some poor fellow called Slow Mando broke a leg. That was the only injury—to men.

The injury to the ships was great. It was no greater than the injury to my feelings. Sentimental nonsense to feel this way about mere creations of wood and canvas? Of course. Even though they would have carried an army to ravage my home; still, I could not remain unaffected. So, I spoke half aloud.

"As I said, let Opaz take care of my conscience."

Pompino glared up. "Opaz?"

The voller steadied on course and I knew Dayra had put on the ropes to control the levers and in a moment or two she appeared in the fighting gallery. She was smiling.

"I did not see you missed one!"

"I do not think there are any left."

"By Vox! What a day!"

Pompino swiveled to look at her. "Ros Delphor? Vox?"

I said: "Poor Pompino lost his famous *Tuscurs Maiden* down there."

Dayra, it was evident, shared my sentimental nonsense about ships only so far. "So Pompino lost a ship. You can always find him another—"

I nodded. "That is true." I looked at Pompino. "How would you like a real Galleon of Vallia, Pompino the Iarvin?"

Now Scauro Pompino was a Khibil. He was smart, shrewd, quick. His foxy face congealed. His shoulders twitched where the ropes bound him, and I knew he wanted to brush up his whiskers. I unsheathed my sailor knife and stepped forward.

"You have always considered yourself the leader in our partnership, Pompino, and that has seemed to me to be just and useful. But when I cut you free, if you attempt to fight me, I think both you and I know you will come off worst."

The ropes fell away.

He stretched and shivered. He put a hand to his whiskers, and then stopped himself. He spoke with an effort.

"I think—" He swallowed and started over. "The Everoinye—they would not be deceived. Perhaps I have known for a long time and would not admit what seemed impossible."

"Now look, Pompino. You and I are good comrades. We're been in plenty of tight scrapes. We've each fought for the other. You like to get away from your lady wife because of reasons. And, I can tell you this, you don't get much fun being a stay-at-home emperor. Believe me."

"Oh, yes, Jak Leemsjid—Dray Prescot—I believe you!"
I eyed him warily. Would he start the full-inclining and
bowing and scraping? Had I lost a good comrade?

He was a smart and foxy devil. He said, "When do I get
the Vallian Galleon?"

Dayra let rip an almighty guffaw.

"I'm going to repaint this airboat and destroy the
Menaham flags. Then I'm going down to Pando and make
sure he sets his army in motion against Kov Colun
Mogper. After that I'll probably have time to nip across
to Vallia. If you can wait until then, why, then, I'll find
you the best galleon the yards of Vallia can build."

"If I can't wait?"

"I think you will. But there will be time for Ros Delphor
to fly you across to Vallia. You'll have to make up your
mind—"

"Oh, I've made up my mind already. I know when I'm
on to a good thing. If we continue as we have, burning
temples to Lem the Silver Leem, following the dictates of
the Everoinye, then I see no reason for a drastic change."

Well, as they say, don't expect a river to change course
just because you throw in a boulder. Even a boulder of
the size I had just thrown.

I nodded. "Good. And remember, Pompino, it is Jak
Leemsjid, as ever."

"As ever."

Moving away ready to go aloft and resume control,
Dayra passed me, and whispered, "He hasn't really taken
it in yet. When he does—"

"He isn't called the Iarvin for nothing."

Dayra swung away going nimbly up the ladder and I
sighed and thought of Delia . . . Delia. . . .

Well, as soon as we'd sorted out Pando, which should
not take long now, and done more about the Lemmites, I
could go back to Vallia and find Delia and tell her what
had happened.

There would be a fine spanking galleon to prepare for
Pompino, too. . . .

Just how would he take this revelation that his comrade was Dray Prescot, Emperor of Vallia?

Then I smiled. Far more important was what would
Delia make of Pompino the Iarvin!